"Why ...
me wh..."

Jill's voice was challenging. This man was far too perceptive.

"I imagine a girl of your beauty is accustomed to large quantities of masculine admiration. After a week here you might be in need of a man's company," Riordan suggested mockingly. "A casual flirtation to keep in practice."

"And I'm supposed to have tricked you into coming with me for that purpose?" Jill demanded.

"You've picked a romantic setting," he taunted. "A walk in the moonlight, just the two of us...alone."

Jill swallowed involuntarily. "If that's my intention, surely I'd have picked a man who at least was attracted to me? You've made your dislike very clear," she answered boldly.

"But I am attracted to you," he said. "I may think you're a scheming little witch—but that doesn't lessen the desire to make love to you!"

JANET DAILEY AMERICANA

BIG SKY COUNTRY

Harlequin Books

TORONTO • NEW YORK • LONDON
AMSTERDAM • PARIS • SYDNEY • HAMBURG
STOCKHOLM • ATHENS • TOKYO • MILAN
MADRID • WARSAW • BUDAPEST • AUCKLAND

The state flower depicted on the cover of this book is bitterroot.

Janet Dailey Americana edition published June 1987
Second printing June 1988
Third printing June 1989
Fourth printing July 1990
Fifth printing September 1991
Sixth printing February 1992

ISBN 0-373-89876-2

Harlequin Presents edition published September 1980
Second printing July 1981

Original hardcover edition published in 1977
by Mills & Boon Limited

BIG SKY COUNTRY

CHAPTER ONE

"KERRY?" Jill Randall tipped her head around the bathroom door, golden curls falling over one shoulder.

A faint smile touched the corners of her glossed lips at the sight of her roommate. Kerry Adams was sitting in the middle of one single bed, a pillow clutched tightly in her arms as she stared dreamily into space. The blonde's smile became impish. Slipping a towel from the bathroom rack, Jill wadded it up and hurled it at her roommate. It landed harmlessly on top of her head.

"Kerry, you're supposed to be getting ready!" Jill stood poised in the doorway, a hand resting on a slim but fully curved hip, her blue eyes laughing at the girl's dazed expression.

The towel was dragged away from its haphazard position on her head, drawing with it strands of straight brown hair, silky and shimmering like satin.

"Must I?" Kerry sighed. Then she pushed her petite frame from the bed and walked restlessly to the window, pushing aside the curtain to gaze outside. "I wish Todd was coming over tonight."

Jill shook her head and stepped back in front of the

bathroom mirror. "Unless you want to fail English lit, you'd better hope Todd doesn't come over."

"I know, but—" a fervent note crept into her roommate's voice "—but I keep thinking I'm going to wake up and find it's all been a dream. That it never really happened."

The teasing glint remained in Jill's eyes as she carefully used the sandy brown pencil to define her light brows more clearly. "Kerry, it's only your *first* proposal."

"And my last! Oh, Jill—" Kerry was in the doorway, a frightened happiness lighting a radiant glow in her otherwise undistinguished face "—Todd asked me to marry him. To be his wife."

"I know, love. You told me that before." Jill's sensual mouth curved into a wide smile that laughed gently at Kerry. They had been roommates for too long for Kerry to take offense.

"I have to keep repeating it or I'll stop believing that it actually happened. I'm not beautiful like you. I couldn't believe it when he asked me out that first time—or the second or the third or the fourth. But I never dreamt . . . . Oh, I did dream about it, but I never believed he could actually be serious about me! He never said so much as one word about the way he felt the other night."

"Didn't I tell you it would work?" Jill winked broadly.

Kerry draped the towel over the rack, a regretful look stealing over her features. A heavy dose of guilty conscience dimmed the light in her brown eyes.

"I still don't know if I should have told him such an outright lie. I haven't got any intentions of leaving Montana to get a job, not even for the summer."

"But Todd didn't know that," Jill reminded her, switching the pencil to the other eyebrow. "Besides, you didn't actually tell him you'd accepted a job out of state, did you?"

"No, I just said that your uncle in California said we could come and work at his resort this summer."

"Then it wasn't a lie, was it? Uncle Peter did write to say we had jobs there if we wanted them." There was an expressive shrug of her shoulders as she maintained her concentration on the image in the mirror. "All you did was fib a little about whether you were accepting the offer or not."

"I suppose so," Kerry sighed and leaned heavily against the door frame. Absently her hand reached up, separating a strand of dark hair from the others to twist it around her finger. "It's just that when you love someone it doesn't seem fair to do all this maneuvering to trick him into doing what you want."

"Todd loves you. He probably would have eventually got around to popping the question. You simply adjusted the timetable in your favor. You'd made it so obvious that you were in love with him. It was only just that you find a way to make him declare his feelings."

The first sentence was the only one Kerry heard. "I'll never be able to understand why Todd Riordan would love me. He should marry someone like you who's beautiful and witty, not someone shy and average like me."

Jill tipped her head to the side, her honey gold hair curling about her shoulders. Her long hair was expensively clipped to achieve that studied style of tousled disarray that only the very beautiful can carry off.

"On the outside, Kerry, you may be the average all-American girl, with your brown eyes and brown hair. Your face and figure might not be spectacular, but inside you're a very beautiful person. Opposites always attract, anyway. Todd Riordan has a very strong protective instinct and your innate shyness brings it to the fore. Plus I think he likes the way you worship him with those brown eyes of yours."

There was more on the tip of her tongue that Jill didn't say, but she thought it to herself. Todd liked the idea that he was intellectually superior to Kerry. He needed someone he could dominate—never domineer, since he wasn't the type. Jill had always guessed that the woman he married would be a brown moth, not a butterfly.

He was a very ambitious young man. It wasn't that he would have objected to sharing the spotlight with a beautiful wife. He wasn't that self-centered. But Todd Riordan wanted to be certain in his own mind that his wife was sitting at home waiting for him without a gaggle of admirers ready and willing to amuse her in the event he was late coming home.

Kerry's ego was very fragile and Jill had spoken the truth when she had said that Kerry was a beautiful person inside. Not for anything would she intentionally hurt her friend by pointing out some of the more callous reasons why Todd Riordan wanted her for his wife.

"I wish you wouldn't talk like that, Jill," Kerry frowned, twisting the lock of hair tighter around her fingers. "You sound so cynical when you do."

"I prefer to think of it as being logical and realistic." Her lashes were already long and curling, but they needed a coating of brown to better define them. Jill artfully stroked the mascara brush. "Men are tall little boys. Oh, they each have their own personality, but inside they're still little boys. Once a female recognizes that fact and treats men accordingly, she's already the winner. All you have to do, Kerry, is praise them when they're good; withhold their treats when they're bad; and play their games when there's something you want them to do for you."

"That's easy for you to say. There isn't any man you can't have if you want him." A faintly envious note crept into Kerry's voice as she studied the exquisitely feminine features of her roommate—features that could change from sensually alluring to innocently young with hardly a blink of an eye in between.

"That's true," Jill agreed matter-of-factly. The mascara brush halted in midstroke, the rich azure color of her eyes deepening when she glanced self-consciously at Kerry's reflection in the mirror. "Lawdy, that sounded conceited, didn't it? I didn't mean it that way."

"You're not conceited, just confident. If I looked

like you, I probably would be, too. As it is, I'm just glad you don't want Todd."

The strand of dark hair was released, Kerry's voice trailing away as she moved into the bedroom they shared. Automatically Jill resumed the application of mascara to her lashes.

"You are going to change into everyday clothes before going to the library, aren't you?" she inquired absently.

"Just a sweatshirt and jeans," was the shrugging response.

With the mascara brush returned to the orderly row of cosmetics, Jill stared at her reflection for long moments. She was never startled by the beautiful girl that stared back at her. It was the same face she had always seen. She had been born a butterfly. From almost the beginning she had been the object of many little boys' attentions.

It was true—she could have any man she wanted. Some were more a challenge than others, but they all could be got. It was merely a matter of playing a game. Sometimes Jill thought of herself as more of a chameleon than a butterly, changing into whatever personality the man she was snaring wanted her to be. Sexy, sporty, fragile, intellectual, it made no difference.

Jill never once doubted that she could take Todd away from Kerry if she wanted him. She could appear as helpless and naïve as Kerry actually was. With Todd, her beauty would be a handicap, but she could turn that around and show him what an advantage her looks would be to his career. She would never do it. Kerry was the best friend Jill had ever had, and Kerry loved Todd desperately.

Had she ever looked at a man with Kerry's love-starred eyes? The mist of pink hearts had never lasted beyond the initial infatuation that attracted her to a particular man. Once she had him in her grasp, her power so to speak, the infatuation disintegrated. The thrill of the chase always excited her, but the actual kill Jill found boring.

A long-sleeved white blouse was on the hanger on the back of the bathroom door. Jill slipped it on, buttoning it from the bottom up, watching the cotton material discreetly accent the thrust of her breasts.

A butterfly was an apt description of herself. A golden Monarch flitting from man to man, never dallying anywhere too long. Was this destined to be her life cycle, or would some man come along to clip her wings?

That was a fanciful thought. From birth she had known instinctively how to get around any man. There wasn't one she couldn't eventually get to do what she wanted. Once she had him dancing attendance on her, she simply spread her wings and flew away.

With a shrug that such thoughts were a waste of time, Jill tucked her blouse into the waistband of her powder blue denims. Fingers absently fluffed the burnished ends of her hair as she stepped from the bathroom to the bedroom.

"Ready?" Kerry tugged a yellow windbreaker over her faded gray sweatshirt. The overall effect was a tomboyish appearance that suited the bobbed hair style and average face, but wasn't at all complimentary to her true personality.

Jill noted all this with an absent, appraising eye, but she had long ago given up trying to persuade her roommate to dress differently. Kerry had achieved a marriage proposal from the man she loved, so Jill guessed that it didn't really make much difference.

"Who is ever ready to do research on a term paper?" Her fawn-colored leather jacket was taken from the small closet, a twin to the one that held Kerry's clothes.

"Look at it this way," Kerry laughed. "A term-paper deadline means the end of another term and summer vacation around the corner."

Jill swept up her notebooks and bag, walking to the door her roommate held open for her. "That's a cheerful thought," she agreed with a wide smile.

"How soon are you going to be using the typewriter?"

The question by Kerry started a comparison of schedules between the two as they descended the stairs leading to the entrance hall. The used portable typewriter had been a joint investment, but their need to use it invariably occurred at the same time.

A girl appeared at the base of the stairs, took two quick steps, glanced up, then paused at the sight of the two girls coming down.

"There you are, Jill. I was just coming upstairs to get you. You have a phone call ... sounds like Bob Jackson."

The breathless announcement ended with a conspiratorial grin before the girl turned around to retrace her steps. Jill concealed a grimace. Bob Jackson was a recent conquest, one she was now trying to fly away from. He couldn't seem to take the hint.

"Tell him I'll be right there," Jill called after the retreating girl and hurried her steps.

"He's persistent," Kerry murmured.

"Don't I know it!" A brow was arched briefly in her direction. "This shouldn't take long, though."

The girl who had come to get her pointed to the telephone booth in the entrance hall. Jill walked quickly toward it while Kerry settled into the lumpy cushion of the sofa nearby. A hurried busy tone was easy to adopt.

"Hi, Jill. What are you doing?" The male voice belonging to Bob Jackson responded to her rushed greeting.

"Oh, Bob, it's you. I was just on my way to the library with Kerry trying to finish up the notes for my term paper. Talk about leaving things to the last minute! It's due on Monday, you know, and I've hardly begun."

"Oh." There was a hesitating pause and Jill knew her statement did not coincide with his plans for the weekend. "All work and no play makes Jill a dull girl," he offered in tentative jest. "We're having a dance this Saturday, remember?"

"If this Jill doesn't get her term paper done, she's going to flunk." It was a plausible excuse, although

Jill was fully aware that it was not going to take her
the entire weekend to complete the paper.

A night out would not hurt anything. She simply
didn't want to spend it with Bob. Besides, Kerry had
mentioned that the three of them—Kerry, Todd and
Jill—might go out to dinner this weekend, a miniature
engagement party.

Her roommate was sensitive about the fact that she
had no family except for an aunt and uncle in Billings
who had raised her when her parents died. Kerry
never said anything specific, but Jill had sensed it had
not been a mutually happy arrangement.

"What's one little evening going to hurt?" Bob
wheedled. "Come on, honey. We'll have a great
time."

The front door was slammed shut. Jill glanced
automatically toward the noise. Absently she made
some objection to Bob's statement as she stared curiously at the stranger who had made such a loud
entrance.

Her gaze swept over his appearance, taking in the
sheepskin-lined suede parka unbuttoned to the cool-
ness of the late spring night. Dark blue levis hugged
slim hips and long legs, stopping on the arches of a
pair of cowboy boots, dirty and worn with much use.
Yet there was something about his erect bearing that
said he wasn't an ordinary cowboy off the range.

Bob was saying something again and Jill let her
gaze fall away from the stranger to concentrate on
what was being said in her ear. Then the stranger's
voice penetrated the glass walls of the booth.

"I was told I could find Kerry Adams here."

The announcement was made to Connie Dickson, the same girl who had come to let Jill know about her telephone call. Jill's blue eyes darted swiftly back to the man, watching as Connie pointed to Kerry sitting on the sofa. Jill would have sworn she knew everyone that Kerry was even briefly acquainted with, but this man who had asked for her roommate was a total stranger.

The harsh planes of his face were impassive as he passed the telephone booth where Jill stood. His long strides reminded Jill of the restless pacing of a caged jungle cat, impatient and angry. This man wasn't as calm as his expression indicated. The hard line of his mouth was too grim. The way his gaze narrowed on her unsuspecting roommate gave Jill the uncomfortable feeling that he had just sighted his prey. There wasn't any way she could warn Kerry.

Jill didn't even pretend to pay attention to the male voice on the telephone. Her hearing was straining to catch what that man was saying to her friend.

"Kerry Adams?" He towered above her, his low voice clipped and abrupt as his earlier demand had been. Cold arrogance crackled through the tension that held him motionless. There was no flicker of recognition in Kerry's startled upward glance. "I'm Todd's brother."

Jill's eyes widened in surprise. Outside of both men being dark complected the comparison ended there. Vaguely she had been aware that Todd had an older

brother. Kerry had mentioned it at some time, or
perhaps Todd had himself.

"Of course, how . . . how do you d-do," Kerry
stammered uncertainly.

Her petite frame quickly straightened from the
couch to stand in front of the man, momentarily
forgetting the notebooks on her lap until they clattered to the floor, loose pages sliding across the
linoleum.

Jill's mouth tightened as she watched Kerry's fum-
bling attemps to recover them, cheeks flaming in
embarrassment and the man making no attempt to
help in the recovery. He uttered not one diplomatic
word to ease Kerry's discomfort nor did he smile to
take away the humiliation of such awkwardness. He
simply waited with thinning patience until Kerry had
retrieved the papers and had them clutched defen-
sively against her chest.

"T-Todd has talked about you often, Mr. Riordan."
Kerry seemed unable to maintain the man's gaze, her
look helplessly falling away.

Standing, the man dwarfed her petite frame oddly
dwarfing it more completely than when Kerry had
been sitting on the sofa.

The tentative comment of friendship was ignored.
"Todd called me this morning. He said he'd asked you
to marry him."

The disbelief . . . no, Jill recognized it was more
than disbelief. It was cutting contempt that sliced
through his words. Kerry swallowed convulsively.

"He did." The admission was made in a tiny voice

that was humbly apologetic. If possible, the man Riordan's expression became grimmer and more forbidding.

"When do you graduate, Miss Adams?" he challenged coldly.

"I . . . I have one more y-year."

His voice became harshly soft. Jill held her breath in an effort to hear him. "Todd has three, possibly four more years before he obtains his final law degree. Am I to support you as well as my brother for that period of time?"

Kerry seemed to shrink visibly away from him. Dominating bully! Jill swore angrily beneath her breath. He was domineering, she corrected her choice of words quickly. That man would use physical strength to impress his will on someone else if need be. Women were the weaker sex, an easy target. Shy, timid Kerry didn't have a chance against his slashing sarcasm.

"Bob, I have to go," Jill spoke hurriedly into the phone, her temper seething as she uncaringly interrupted him. "Call me tomorrow."

As she hung up the receiver, her mind buzzed with the courses of action available to rescue her best friend. Any attempt to argue on Kerry's behalf would be wasted. That man would never listen to a woman's logic, however right it might be. No doubt he considered a woman had only two places in life, in the kitchen and the bedroom. Beyond that, she should be seen and not heard.

Her eyes narrowed for a fleeting moment, a tiny

smile of satisfaction edging the corners of her mouth. Very well, Jill thought, he believed women were silly, simpering creatures. She was about to give him a double dose!

Pushing open the folding door of the telephone booth, Jill stepped out, wrapping her arms around her notebooks and holding them to her chest. She paused, adopted her best "dumb blonde" look and walked forward to engage her opponent.

"Hi, Kerry. I'm ready now," she called brightly to her roommate.

She was completely blind to the stricken look from Kerry. She couldn't allow one flicker of concern to cloud her blue eyes at the total lack of color in her friend's face. Her deliberately innocent eyes swept to the man.

Although braced for his look of displeasure, she was jolted by his piercing gaze. Shards of silver gray splintered over her face before he glanced away, dismissing her as being of little importance. Jill blinked for an instant to retain her poise. The jet blackness of his hair and brows had not prepared her to meet a pair of eyes of metallic gray.

A frightened, helpless confusion gripped Kerry. Her beseeching brown eyes riveted themselves to Jill's face. Jill tried to instill a warmth of reassurance in her smile that gently prodded for an introduction. It took an instant for the bewildered Kerry to understand.

"I . . . I'd like you to meet m-my roommate, m-my friend, Jillian Randall." Her shaking voice wavered traitorously. "Thi . . . This is Todd's brother." A wave of red engulfed Kerry's face. "I'm so . . . sorry, but I don't know your first name, Mr. Riordan."

"Riordan is sufficient."

A cigarette was between his lips, a darkly tanned hand cupping a match to the end. The clipped indifference was reinforced by the lack of a glance in Jill's direction.

"Mr. Riordan, this is really a pleasure to meet you." Jill wasn't about to offer a hand in greeting. As rude as he was, he would ignore it, and she didn't intend to let herself to be cut like that. "And please call me Jill. All my friends do." The quicksilver sheen of his eyes passed over her face briefly and impatiently, openly wishing her gone. It only increased Jill's resolve to remain. "I bet I know why you're here, Mr. Riordan." She smiled widely, darting a warm glance at Kerry, whose face was again drained of color. "You must have heard the news about Kerry and Todd. Isn't it wonderful?"

There was a speaking glance from Riordan that told her to shut up and get lost. Jill's assumed air of denseness naturally didn't understand.

"Everyone here is so envious of Kerry," she rushed on with false excitement. "When you see Todd and Kerry together, it makes you feel all warm and wonderful inside. They're so very much in love it just shines like a golden light. And Todd is so protective of her. No one dares to say a word against Kerry in front of him. You'll really be proud of him, Mr. Riordan, when you see the way he stands up for her."

Put that in your pipe and smoke it, Jill thought

silently. It might be his plan too break up the engagement, but she was confident that Todd would not be as
easy to browbeat as Kerry was. His brother's gaze
narrowed on Jill's guileless expression.

"Miss Randall!" Impatiently he snapped the words
out, cigarette smoke swirling about his face, darkening his eyes to thunderclouds.

Jill spared a silent wish that he could be more aware
of her blond looks, but he seemed impervious to any
attraction to her beauty.

"Jill," she interrupted quickly before he could
finish the statement that was undoubtedly intended to
dismiss her. "I think it's really terrific that you came
all the way into town to meet your brother's fiancée.
The two of you must be very close. How long are you
going to stay?"

He dragged deeply on his cigarette, holding his
temper in check with difficulty as he gazed through
the smoke veil at Kerry.

"Until I've completed what I came to do," he
answered cryptically.

Jill wondered to herself namely, break things up
between Kerry and Todd? Indignation flashed
through her that he should decide without meeting
Kerry that he didn't want her as a sister-in-law.

She released the anger that rose in her throat
through a soft laugh, letting the battling sparkle in her
blue eyes be misinterpreted as happiness.

"That means you can go out to dinner with us
tomorrow night," she declared gaily. His glowering
frown made her rush the explanation that was honey

sweet with satisfaction. "Kerry, Todd and I are going out to dinner on Saturday to celebrate their engagement. Kerry doesn't have any family except an aunt and uncle. I feel as if she's my sister—we've more or less adopted each other. It's a pretend family celebration. You lost your parents, too, didn't you, Mr. Riordan? So it's just you and Todd. Now all four of us can have dinner tomorrow and toast the newly engaged couple. Or did you bring your wife along, Mr. Riordan?" Deliberately she blinked her long, curling lashes at his impassively hard expression.

"I don't have a wife, Miss Randall," in a voice that plainly implied that it was truly none of her business.

Jill tipped her head back, swirling tawny gold hair about her shoulders, purring laughter rising in her throat. "I'll bet you'll be an uncle, then, before you're even a father. And the name is Jill."

His gaze trailed over her blankly happy expression to her throat. Jill was consumed by the sensation that he would like to shake her until her teeth fell out. Kerry moved uneasily beside her.

Jill let her blue gaze swing to her roommate. Her knuckles were turning white with the death grip she had on the notebooks, loose pages sticking out in crumpled disarray. Not even Jill's presence and monopolization of the conversation was regaining Kerry's poise. She was on the verge of breaking, tears welling in her spaniel eyes.

Jill reached out, taking her roommate's left wrist and twisting it to see the watch face. "Look how late it is, Kerry!" she exclaimed, turning an innocently apologetic glance to Todd's brother. "We have our term papers to finish by Monday and mounds of research notes to take. We aren't going to have much time before the library closes." After releasing Kerry's wrist, she dug her fingers into her roommate's shoulder, already turning her away toward the front door. "You'll probably be getting together with Todd. He'll fill you in on what time we're all meeting for dinner tomorrow night. I'm really glad I had the chance to meet you. I know you're just as happy about these two as I am. Good night, Mr. Riordan."

Her cheery departing wave was returned by a look that was broodingly thoughtful. Jill could feel his wintry gray eyes following their path to the door. She kept up a steady, one-sided chatter until the door was safely closed behind them. Only then did she slacken their pace, drinking in deep gulps of the serene evening air.

The palms of her hands were wet. How strange, Jill thought, wiping the nervous perspiration on the hips of her light blue denims. She couldn't remember any time when she had been consciously or unconsciously intimidated by a man. This arrogant Riordan man had affected her more than she realized. Her gaze slid to Kerry, still visibly trembling from the encounter.

"So. That's Todd's older brother," Jill breathed aloud.

Her statement released Kerry from the nameless fear that had held her speechless. Rounded eyes like dark saucers in a pale face swung around to stare at the blonde.

"Oh, Jill, he doesn't want me to marry Todd!" Hysteria strained at the edges of her voice. The dream of perfect love had turned into a nightmare. "Before you got there he told me that if I truly loved Todd, I wouldn't hold him to the proposal. He said Todd still had to finish his education and begin his career and that I shouldn't saddle him with the burden of a wife."

"That's a lot of garbage," Jill responded calmly. Her shoulders lifted beneath the fawn leather jacket to indicate that he didn't know what he was talking about. "There are a lot of women who put their husbands through college. It happens all the time. Todd isn't so extraordinary that you can't do it for him."

"Todd is a Riordan," Kerry whispered, "and I could tell by the look in Riordan's eyes that he didn't think I was a suitable wife for Todd." She paused for a fleeting second. "Do you know, I've never heard Todd call him by his name. He either refers to him as his brother or simply as Riordan."

Jill glanced over her shoulder and saw Riordan emerge from the building. "Let's cut across the grass." She tucked a hand quickly under Kerry's elbow and guided her off the sidewalk. "And I certainly wouldn't worry whether Todd's brother thinks you'll make a suitable wife. It's only Todd's opinion that counts. He must think you will or he would never have proposed to you."

"But I tricked him into that. I made him think I was leaving Montana for the entire summer and we wouldn't see each other until the term started. I shouldn't have done that." Kerry's voice trailed off lamely, heavy with guilt and recrimination.

"What does it matter when Todd proposed to you—now or next fall? Unless you think he might have waited three or four years until he had his degree safely in his hand and a job lined up? And if that Riordan man really does think you aren't suitable, I doubt if time would change his opinion."

The wind tossed a burnished gold strand across Jill's face and she quickly smoothed it back. Her suggestion that Kerry fib about her summer plans might not have been exactly fair, but Jill wasn't going to waste time feeling guilty about it nor allow Kerry to either.

"Do you think Todd knows his brother is in town?" asked Jill in an afterthought.

As much as she disliked it, Jill thought she had to consider the possibility that Todd was having second thoughts about the marriage proposal and was using his brother as an excuse to break it off.

"I had the feeling that Riordan came straight to see me without talking to Todd except for this morning," Kerry answered.

Jill whispered a silent prayer of relief. There might have been some things about Todd that didn't appeal to her personally, but she had always believed his affection for Kerry was honest and straightforward.

"When we get to the library," Jill breathed in deeply, speaking aloud the battle plan that was form-ing in her mind, "I think you should call Todd and let him know in a diplomatic way what happened tonight."

"No." Kerry shook her head, the dark brown bob of straight hair swinging vigorously across her cheeks.

"No?" Jill's blue eyes widened in stunned surprise as she stopped to stare at her roommate. "Why not, for heaven's sake? He is your fiancé."

"But I'm not going to make trouble between Todd and his brother. We haven't been engaged for one whole day yet. I don't want to go running to him just because I might have misunderstood Riordan," her roommate argued.

Jill wondered if it was logic that made Kerry reluctant to go to Todd or an inner fear that Todd might be swayed by his brother's arguments.

"What about dinner tomorrow night?" Jill challenged softly.

"Todd . . . Todd is going to call me in th-the morning. I'll find out what time he thinks the f-four of us should meet." Her wavering voice indicated that her previous argument hadn't changed her apprehensions. She was unsure of Todd's reaction and wanted to postpone the moment when she would find out.

The desire was strong to insist that Kerry call Todd immediately, but Jill subdued it. Her roommate was already subconsciously regretting her interference that had prompted the proposal. She had better sit back and be ready to pick up the pieces or with luck catch Kerry before she fell.

"In between now and tomorrow night—" Jill made her voice nonchalant "—why don't you tell me everything you know about Todd's brother?"

CHAPTER TWO

THE SUM TOTAL of Kerry's knowledge regarding Todd's brother could be numbered on the fingers of one hand, Jill discovered. He was Todd's elder by about eight years, which made him thirty-two or three. He had inherited the family ranch when their father passed away some five years ago. Kerry had forgotten where it was located except that it was somewhere near Dillon, Montana. Beyond that, Kerry couldn't fill in the blanks.

The eraser end of the pencil tapped the edge of her notebook with monotonous rhythm. Only half of Jill's mind was concentrating on the paragraph she was reading. The rest was thinking of Riordan.

Only a fraction of an inch might separate the heights of the two brothers. Again, the similarity stopped there. Todd was supplely lean and his brother was muscled with broad shoulders tapering to a slim waist to give an impression of leanness.

Taken separately, their facial features were much alike. The clean cut of the cheekbones, the sharply defined jawline, the Roman boldness of the nose, the intelligent forehead. The mouths were different. Todd's was curved and mobile, ready to spring into a smile or a laugh. His brother's was hard and grim, nothing gentle about it at all.

The result was night and day. Warm sunshine spilled over Todd to illuminate a smoothly handsome face. The dark shadows of night threw his brother's features in sharp relief to make him strikingly male but never handsome.

Jill leaned against the straight back of the chair, giving up the pretense of interest in the book opened before her. Tonight Riordan had been angry about the engagement of his brother, yet he had seemed curiously detached at the same time. How could a man confront his brother's fiancée with the hope of breaking the engagement and remain aloof at the same time? It was a contradiction of emotion.

A sideways glance at Kerry caught her gazing into space, a hollow look of apprehension in her expression. Jill breathed in deeply and expelled the air in a long sigh. Neither of them had accomplished anything in the two hours they had spent at the library.

The pages of her notebook were flipped shut with an air of finality. "Let's call it a night, Kerry," she murmured so as not to disturb the others studying at the long table.

Without a whisper of protest, Kerry gathered her papers trancelike into a stack and followed Jill out of the library.

A round silver-dollar moon hung above the capital city of Montana, its silvery light touching the crowning peaks of the mountains surrounding the city. A cool night breeze ruffled the careless wings of tawny hair at Jill's temples, the golden color paled by the moonlight. A crisscrossing spider web of streetlights illuminated the sidewalks and the girls walking in tense silence.

The whisper of tires on pavement went unnoticed until a car rolled to a stop beside them, the passenger door opening to block their progress. Kerry was nearest to the street. It was on her the pair of steel gray eyes focused.

"Get in. I'll give you a ride," was the curt command.

Riordan again! He must have been waiting outside the library for them to leave, Jill decided swiftly as Kerry remained frozen in her tracks. The invitation was meant for her roommate alone and Jill knew it. Riordan intended to have his talk with Kerry, and Jill knew of only one way to circumvent it.

"Why, Mr Riordan! We didn't expect to see you out here waiting for us." Jill stepped quickly forward, a bright smile curving her mouth. "How thoughtful of you to offer us a ride. Studying can be so mentally exhausting that it just drains all your energy." As she slipped into the passenger seat, she avoided the gaze that tried to impale her on the pair of steel sabers. "A person can tell you're Todd's brother. He's always doing thoughtful things like this."

Only when she was seated and about to make room for the bewildered Kerry did Jill allow her innocent blue eyes to be caught by his gaze. The line of his mouth was forbiddingly harsh. She let her eyes widen and the smile fade from her lips. "Oh," she murmured in a very tiny voice, "you were only going to take Kerry, weren't you? You didn't mean to give me a ride, too. I am sorry, Mr. Riordan. I didn't mean to be so obtuse. You want to talk to Kerry alone, don't you?"

"If it wouldn't inconvenience you greatly, Miss Randall, I would," he agreed with cynical tautness.

"It's all right." Jill began sliding out of the car, making her shoulders give a falsely self-conscious shrug. "It isn't all that far to walk. I've done it lots of times, although never at night and alone."

As Jill stepped from the car, Kerry's gaze clung beseechingly to her face. Jill smiled faintly, not giving her roommate the reassurance she wanted.

"You go ahead and ride with Mr. Riordan," she prompted gently. "I'll see you back at our room."

"Jill, no, not alone!" The frightened protest was to voice Kerry's apprehension at being alone with Todd's brother.

Jill deliberately misunderstood her. "Don't be silly, Kerry. I'm not going to be molested. Except for that one block, it's all very well lit. I'll be okay, really."

As she expected, Kerry still didn't get into the car, hesitating while she silently pleaded for Jill to rescue her. From inside the car, Riordan swore under his breath.

"Both of you get in!" he snapped.

Her back was to the open door and Jill winked broadly at Kerry. It was difficult to conceal her smile of triumph, although she knew it was only a temporary one.

She urged Kerry to get in the car first while her mind raced for a way to rescue her friend once they arrived at their destination. There wasn't any chance that she would be able to sit in the car and take part in the discussion as she had done in the hallway.

As they pulled away from the curb, a silence settled in, threatening to become oppressive. An uncontrollable shiver quaked over Kerry's shoulders, signaling to Jill that she couldn't let Riordan's presence dominate them.

"I guess it's the romantic in me that always finds weddings so exciting." Jill heard the sound of disgust that came from Riordan's throat and smiled securely in the darkness of the car. "Kerry has already promised that I can be her maid of honor. I know Todd will ask you to be his best man. That's why I'm so glad I've had this chance to meet you before the wedding." She rushed on, "We've been talking about what colors Kerry should choose. She wants green and yellow. They are her favorites, but I was thinking it should be yellow and white or green and white. What's your opinion, Mr. Riordan?" she asked, leaning forward as if she was really interested in his answer, then hurrying on before he could reply. "I guess it really depends on when they decide to get married. Yellow and white would hardly be good winter colors, although I doubt if they would wait that long before tying the knot."

The inanity of her chatter sickened Jill. She knew it reinforced Riordan's opinion that she was a silly dumb blonde. At the moment she was interested only in shielding Kerry for as long as she could. All too soon the short distance was traveled from the library to their dormitory.

The car stopped in front of the building. Unable to meet Kerry's pleading eyes, Jill glanced around her roommate to the impassive profile of the driver.

"Thank's a lot for the ride, Mr. Riordan," she offered brightly, and received a curt nod of dismissal in reply.

A quick good night to Kerry and Jill was out of the car. She wanted to run to the front door, but she kept her steps unhurried. The instant the door was closed behind her, she raced for the telephone booth.

Excitement had her fingers shaking. Jill had to try twice before she dialed the number correctly. "Todd Riordan, please, and hurry!" Her voice was oddly breathless. She curled her fingers in the coil of the telephone receiver as she waited impatiently.

"Todd Riordan here," came his familiar male voice.

"Todd, this is Jill."

"Jill?" His surprise was obvious. "What's wrong? Is something the matter with Kerry?"

"Yes, in a way. I haven't much time to explain. Your brother is here."

"Riordan? Damn him!" was the muttered response.

With a flash of insight Jill realized that Riordan had evidently made his opinion of Todd's engagement quite clear when Todd had made the telephone call to inform him of it. At least it didn't mean she had to make a lengthy explanation.

She took a deep breath. She might as well let Todd know that she was aware of his brother's displeasure.

"He and Kerry are outside the house now. I believe he's suggesting that your engagement is unwise. Kerry didn't want you to know about this, so when I go out there to tell her you're on the phone, I want you to pretend you're the one who called and not me."

"I'll take care of it," Todd answered grimly.

Setting the receiver on the small counter of the booth, Jill pivoted sharply out of the glass doors and retraced her path through the front door to the car. Her heart was pounding in her throat as she bent her head toward the window.

"Kerry, Todd's called. He wants to talk to you." In spite of her attempt to relay the message calmly, there was a thread of victory. The sensation was increased by the look of utter relief on her roommate's face.

Kerry nearly bolted out of the car, not offering one word of goodbye to the grim-faced man behind the wheel. Jill couldn't resist a glance at him. There were times when rubbing salt into wounds was very enjoyable.

"Maybe you would like to talk to Todd, Mr. Riordan?" she suggested with saccharine sweetness.

His mouth tightened harshly. "No, Miss Randall, I wouldn't."

The key was turned in the ignition and the powerful engine purred to life. Jill closed the door that Kerry had left open. Satisfaction glittered in her blue eyes as she watched the disappearing taillights that declared her the victor in this round.

At a more leisurely pace, she returned to the building. A glance at the tearfully happy smile on Kerry's face indicated that Todd was doing a very adequate job of reassuring her of his affection.

Riordan's first attempt had been thwarted and Todd was now aware of the attempt. Would Riordan try again? A light brown brow arched faintly in speculation. Yes, he probably would, she decided. Perhaps with Todd involved he wouldn't be nearly as blunt, but she doubted if his determination had lessened.

It wasn't part of Jill's nature to inquire later exactly what Todd had said to Kerry. She and Kerry exchanged a lot of confidences, but her roommate was a very private person when it came to her inner emotions. There were personal aspects of her private life she was too shy to discuss and Jill wouldn't probe

The only sour note in the evening's conclusion was that the dinner the following evening was no longer an uncertainty. Like it or not Jill had to attend. She couldn't plead the excuse that it was a family affair, not after she had bragged about the dinner to Riordan and invited him herself.

When the appointment hour arrived, Jill discovered that she was strangely looking forward to another encounter with Riordan. She attributed it to curiosity. It would be interesting to find out what his tactics would be now that he was presented with a united front. He had failed to divide Kerry from the rest and conquer her. Would he attempt to take on all three of them?

The hotel's wall mirror told Jill she had chosen her clothes well. The simple design of her dress gave her an air of innocent sophistication while the azure color pointed up the purity of blue in her eyes.

Jill caught Todd's warm smile in the mirror and returned it. They were comrades in arms, united to protect the petite, dark-haired girl walking between them.

"Where is he?" There was a tremor of nerves in Kerry's whispered question, her brown eyes sweeping the hotel lobby including its open staircase to locate the man they had come to meet.

Todd's arm tightened slightly around her waist. "Riordan said he'd meet us in the lounge."

"Doesn't your brother have a first name?" Jill focused her attention on the closed lounge door. She half expected him to appear with the striding suddenness of the first time.

"Yes, it's John, but I can't remember the last time anyone called him that. He's always been simply Riordan. And I wouldn't suggest that you call him John either, unless you fancy being turned into a frog. He despises the name."

"John? But that's a good Christian name." Her blue eyes widened in surprise.

"My mother named him after the man she admired most—her father," Todd answered dryly as his hand slipped to Kerry's elbow. He reached around to open the lounge door.

Jill would have liked to pursue that curious statement, but there wasn't time for a discussion of the

Riordan family history. They were inside the lounge and somewhere in the dim room Todd's brother was waiting for them.

Like Todd and Kerry, her eyes searched the scattered occupants of the room. She didn't recognize Riordan among the men sitting at the bar, nor was he sitting at any of the small round tables.

A light flickered in a corner booth, flaring brightly for an instant as a match would. The brief flame cast a golden light over onyx black hair and the darkly tanned, rugged features of the man bending to its light.

Jill felt her senses sharpening immediately. Darting a glance at Todd, she saw by the arch of his brow that he, too, had seen his brother. Meeting her glance above Kerry's head, his hazel brown eyes said, *let's get it over with*. The arm at Kerry's waist turned her towards the booth and the three of them started forward at the same time.

An inner voice told Jill that Riordan had seen them the minute they had entered the lounge, although he didn't visibly acknowledge their presence until they were nearly at the booth. Then he slid with catlike grace to his feet to meet them.

The sheepskin-lined parka was gone. So were the denims and the cowboy boots. Jill realized, too late, that she had been partly taken in by his western garb in their previous meeting.

She had not anticipated the worldliness and sophistication that she saw now. A stranger viewing this Riordan in gray slacks, black blazer and ribbed white turtleneck would see him as a business executive, not a man of the rugged outdoors as Jill had labeled him. She had underestimated him, and it was a mistake she didn't intend to repeat.

The metallic gray eyes ignored both Jill and Kerry as Riordan met the silent challenge of his brother's gaze. Todd resolutely forced him to acknowledge both of them by making formal introductions. The action brought a twisting smile of cynicism to the ruthlessly hard mouth, but the look directed briefly at Jill and Kerry in turn was smoothly without emotion.

"Shall we sit down?" Riordan suggested blandly.

With some misgivings, Jill noted that she was to sit on the booth seat next to Riordan. Naturally Todd wanted to be close to Kerry, although Jill wished he had chosen to sit beside his brother.

The desire to slide as close to the wall as possible was nearly irrepressible. The palms of her hands were beginning to become damp. Jill chided herself to relax and stop being intimidated by the man sitting beside her. She had maneuvered him quite easily yesterday. There was no reason to think she couldn't do it again if the need arose.

To break the silence until the waitress arrived to take their drink order, Todd inquired about the ranch and received ambiguous replies from Riordan. In another second the weather is going to be discussed, Jill thought tensely, darting a quick look at the slightly pale face of her roommate.

After the waitress had their order, Jill could see the impatience building in Todd's face. Riordan wasn't

angry. There was none of the aloof black moodiness
that had been evident yesterday in his expression. In
fact, he seemed quite content with just making them
uneasy.

"May I have a cigarette?" Jill broke in after another vague, uncommunicative response from Riordan to one of Todd's questions.

Todd was reaching into his jacket pocket when the
hand of the man beside her shook a cigarette out of a
pack and offered it to her. Was it amusement she saw
glittering in the gray depths of Riordan's eyes? What
had she done that he found so amusing? He couldn't
possibly guess that her request for a cigarette had
merely been a ploy to soften Todd's tight-lipped
expression and distract his growing anger.

"No, thank you," Jill refused with a demure smile.
Todd's pack was in front of her and she took one from
it. "I prefer filter-tipped cigarettes," she explained
with studied lightness. "The kind you smoke, Mr.
Riordan . . . well, the tobacco always clings to my
lipstick."

His gaze centered on the sensual curve of her lips,
glistening with the moistness of gloss. "I envy the
tobacco," he said dry voiced.

A pulse throbbed in her throat as unwillingly Jill
glanced at the firm line of his mouth, a hint of cruelty
in its masculine hardness. It would be no gentle kiss
that he'd give a woman.

The scrape of a match head was followed by the
pungent scent of burning sulfur. Then his fingers were
cupping the flame and offering it to Jill. Her gaze

skittered away from the gleam of mockery in his eyes. He couldn't possibly read her thoughts, she scolded herself, bending her golden head to touch the tip of the cigarette to the flame.

The drinks arrived, causing a momentary distraction. The more time Jill had to think about Riordan's suggestive remark, the more she realized it had not been an attempt to flirt with her. He wasn't the type to flirt. He had been stating a fact. Men had often complimented her, so why should his casual reference to her beauty disturb her? It didn't make sense.

Her fingers closed around the cold glass in front of her. She smiled across the table at Kerry, who was glancing uncertainly at Todd. The electric current flowing from the man beside her needled Jill. She lifted her glass.

"I'd like to propose a toast," Jill declared. From the corner of her eye she could see Riordan leaning back, almost physically detaching himself from the group. "To the future Mr. and Mrs. Todd Riordan."

A shy pink crept into Kerry's cheeks as she peered at Todd's smiling face through the veil of her dark lashes. The faint reflection of embarrassment made the sparkle of love in her brown eyes all the more radiant.

Three glasses met in the center of the table, but it was the absence of the fourth that was most notable. The gentle smile that had been on Todd's face faded as his gaze clashed and locked with his brother's. Sooty lashes had narrowed to a black screen, throwing shadows to darken the watchful gray eyes.

Todd didn't carry the glass to his mouth. "Rior-dan?" he prompted firmly.

Riordan appeared unmoved by the reprimand at his rudeness. In fact, he appeared very relaxed and in command.

"I've made my disapproval of your engagement quite obvious. Don't expect me to drink to it, Todd," was the bland response.

"It happens to be my life. Surely it's my business what I do with it," challenged Todd.

"Being your brother gives me the right to interfere or at the very least, voice my opinion." The broad shoulders shrugged expressively. "If you are intent on marrying this girl, I can't stop you. But I can and I will withhold my support."

"That's not fair, Riordan, and you know it. That money is mine for my education," Todd snapped.

"It's unfortunate that your father gave me sole control of the trust fund until you're thirty, then, isn't it?" The low voice was lazily calm as Riordan figuratively spread his cards on the table. He held a strong hand.

"It may come as a shock to you, but I think Kerry and I can make it without your support. It will mean sacrifices for both of us, holding down full-time jobs and a full schedule of credits at college, but we can do it." Todd's arm circled Kerry's shoulder, drawing her closer to him.

"And maintain the grade level you have?" Riordan mocked.

"Maybe not, but we would get our degrees."

"I imagine it sounds all very noble to the two of you, struggling together, completely on your own. The harsh fact is that you'll be so busy struggling to survive that it will be four or five years before you realize you've made a mistake. The two of you simply aren't compatible. By that time there might be a child involved. You and I, Todd, know what it's like to grow up with parents that have separated."

"Kerry and I are very compatible and very much in love," Todd disagreed forcefully.

"That's what our parents claimed, too," was the quiet and silencing reply.

Todd wasn't able to hold the level gaze of his brother, a certain indication to Jill that Riordan's remark had touched a vulnerable spot. He let the pregnant silence settle heavily over the table before he continued.

"I'm not trying to make things difficult. I'm trying to appeal to your reason, Todd," he said calmly. "This is not the time in your life to tie yourself down with a wife. Not because you're young—age matters little—but because the next few years you need to devote to your studies and your future career. You can't possibly give the attention your wife would be entitled to receive. Your timing is off, Todd. You're rushing into something with your eyes closed. Open them. Make certain you're not confusing lust with love. Take her to bed. Make her your lover or mistress. But don't be a fool and marry her!"

Kerry's ashen face flamed scarlet. Jill wondered angrily why she had thought Riordan would be any less blunt with the three of them. Todd had started to listen to his brother's arguments, but the disrespect in the last of his statements had fortunately wiped out the inroads Riordan had made. He had overplayed his hand.

"If—" Todd was angry and making no attempt to conceal it "—you'd taken the trouble to get to know Kerry, you wouldn't be so quick to insult her!"

"I've never pretended to be the tactful one in this family." Riordan's mouth twisted into a cold smile to match the glacial color of his eyes. "You'll be wasting energy to defend the girl's honor to me. If you feel the necessity for action, go arrange for a table in the dining room."

There was a seething moment of silence before Todd rose to his feet, impatiently signaling to Kerry to accompany him. Jill was forgotten as the couple exited the lounge. She studied the building ashes on the end of her cigarette, murderous thoughts racing impotently through her mind.

"Well, Miss Randall?" Riordan's quietly challenging voice hadn't forgotten her.

Her eyes were round and blank when she turned to him. "Yes?"

"You're quite obviously in favor of this engagement. Aren't you going to defend your girl friend?" The deceptively soft tone sliced like Toledo steel through silk.

"I wouldn't like to rudely contradict you, but I've seen Todd and Kerry together," Jill murmured with innocent apology. "I've noticed three things about them. There is a physical desire, as one would expect, but their feelings are essentially very strong and tender. And I think their personalities beautifully complement each other and fulfill basic needs."

"Todd takes after our grandfather. His ambitions are political. Can you picture Kerry as a politician's wife? Her shyness, timidity will prove to be a problem in a few years." Jill slowly brushed the ashes off the end of her cigarette, unable to meet the intense scrutiny for fear her eyes would reveal her partial agreement with Riordan's assessment. "Todd should eventually marry someone like you who could be an asset to his chosen career," he concluded.

"Like me?" A genuine frown of confusion puckered her brows, as she tucked a tawny gold strand of hair behind her ear.

"An attractive . . . a beautiful woman to be his hostess and entertain the important people he will have to cultivate."

"Really?" Jill tipped her head to one side as if considering his statement. "It's strange how our opinions vary. Whenever I see a man in public office who has a beautiful wife, I always have the feeling that he's lost touch with the common people. Besides, I think Todd would rather have a wife waiting at home than working beside him."

Again the sooty lashes narrowed, making an unreadable smoke screen of his eyes. "That's a very interesting opinion. You're convinced that a marriage between the two would work."

"I think it would work very well," she affirmed,

trying to be offhand and not forceful with her statement despite her inner convictions.

"Are you in favor of couples marrying while they're still attending college, and, in Todd's case, of Kerry supporting them for a few years while he obtains all his degrees? That's quite a strain on a marriage, don't you agree?"

"Yes." Jill nodded. A sparkle of battle glittered in her blue eyes so she forced a smile to hide the antagonism he aroused. "Of course, if you were more kindly disposed in their favor, it wouldn't be quite as much of a struggle, would it?"

"That's what you think I should do?"

Riordan was leaning back, the ebony color of his hair darkened further by the shadows of the booth, his striking powerful features fully illuminated by the dim light.

The unwavering study of his light-colored eyes made Jill vividly aware of the primitive charm he possessed. Her heartbeat accelerated briefly under the potent spell of his virility.

Averting her head, Jill pretended a concentration in snubbing out her cigarette. She had to break free of the magnetic pull of his gaze.

"I wouldn't presume to tell you what you should do." She laughed softly, giving the impression that the thought was ridiculous that a mere female could influence him one way or the other.

"Wouldn't you?"

The mocking words were said so softly that Jill wasn't sure whether she had heard them or only imagined them. There was no mistake the next time he spoke. His voice was clear and calm.

"But you wouldn't disagree if I said that it's your opinion I should get to know Kerry better before I make my decision irrevocable."

"Of course, I wouldn't disagree with that. There's nothing worse than estrangement between two brothers and I know Kerry would be deeply hurt to be the cause of any more harsh words between you and Todd." That was very definitely the truth. Kerry could be too sensitive. "And I certainly wouldn't want the two of them to do something so foolish as to elope, not when there still might be a chance for your differences to be reconciled."

The wide-eyed, "dumb blond" look was firmly fixed on her face. Arguing with a man as arrogant as Riordan only made him more stubborn. It was better to let him believe that she spoke with the wisdom of the simple and was not trying to threaten him into changing his mind.

A measuring, thoughtful glance trailed over Jill's face. Then Riordan reached for his glass, downed the drink and replaced the empty glass on the table.

"Shall we go in search of Todd and your friend?" he suggested with a side look. "They may have decided to eat without us."

Jill gave a little nod of agreement and waited until he was standing to slide out of the booth. His gaze swept appraisingly over her when she stood at his side, a silver glitter that was faintly mocking. Not a

guiding hand touched her, but she was very much
aware of him walking beside her as they left the
lounge.

CHAPTER THREE

THE CONVERSATION at the dinner table was stilted. It would have taken only a few conciliatory comments from Riordan to ease the tension, but he didn't make them. Jill had thought her comments had made an impression on him. Looking back, she could see it hadn't made any difference in his stand against Kerry's engagement to Todd.

There hadn't been any further confrontations, if that was a consolation. There again Jill decided it was because Riordan believed he had pushed Todd as far as he dared. But if Riordan's aim had been to make Kerry unhappy, he had succeeded. Jill couldn't remember seeing her roommate's face look so pinched and strained. Todd's look of concern and smiles of reassurance weren't as bolstering as they might have been if they were alone.

While Riordan was occupied paying the check, Jill made the decision that Todd and Kerry should be alone. The sooner, the better. She could easily catch a taxi.

"Todd," she spoke quietly, not wanting to draw Riordan's attention, "why don't you and Kerry go ahead and leave? I'll find my own way."

"Are you sure you don't mind?" But the relief was in Todd's eyes.

"I suggested it, didn't I?" Jill smiled. Kerry opened her mouth to protest, but Riordan was moving toward them, his deceptively lazy strides covering the distance swiftly.

The way Todd protectively nestled Kerry deeper in the crook of his arm lifted one corner of his brother's mouth in a mocking smile. It remained there to accept Kerry's frozen goodbye.

"I'll meet you here at seven in the morning for breakfast, Todd, before I leave for the ranch." It wasn't a suggestion, it was a command. Jill's lips started to tighten at his autocratic action, but she relaxed them instantly into a smile when the gray eyes swung to her. "Miss Randall." There was an arrogant inclination of his dark head in goodbye.

"Goodnight, Mr. Riordan." She wasn't about to thank him for a miserable evening.

In the hotel lobby, they parted company, with Riordan disappearing almost immediately, presumably returning to his room. Todd hesitantly suggested that he and Kerry should give Jill a ride, but she airily waved it aside. The pair insisted on waiting until Jill had telephoned the taxi company and received assurances that a cab would be dispatched immediately.

Todd's car was pulling out of the hotel parking lot. Jill stared through the glass windows at the dark shape of Kerry's head resting on the driver's shoulder. The course of true love never did run smooth. Wasn't that the saying? It must be true love, because Todd and Kerry had actually had a bumpy start.

"Don't tell me they forgot to take you with them?"

Jill pivoted sharply, her startled eyes focusing on Riordan. One arm held his jacket open, the hand negligently thrust in his trouser pocket. The other hand held a cigarette to his mouth, his eyes narrowed against the smoke curling from the burning tip.

"Or did you arrange to be left behind?" Riordan added in a mocking taunt.

For another full second, speech was denied her. A hand crept up to her convulsively working throat and she managed a jerky laugh.

"You startled me." Her hair was caught in the collar of her light coat and she pushed it free. "Kerry and Todd weren't going directly back, so I decided to take a taxi. I-I don't like being the spare tire."

Her voice was low and oddly breathless. He surely didn't think she had stayed behind on the offchance of seeing him again.

"I doubt that *you* would," he agreed with biting emphasis on "you." "But there's no need for you to take a cab. I was just going for a drive myself. I'll give you a ride."

"You don't need to do that. There's already a cab on the way here." Frantically Jill glanced out of the window, catching the headlight beam as a car swung up to the curb beneath the covered drive. "In fact it's here now. It was kind of you to offer, though."

Before she could reach for the door handle, his arm was already in front of her to pull it open. Ducking under his arm, Jill unwillingly looked into his coolly appraising gray eyes, reflecting nothing but her own image. The cab driver was approaching the door as she stepped onto the sidewalk with Riordan directly and disconcertingly behind her.

"Did you call for a cab?"

"Yes," Jill responded quickly.

Riordan's hand closed over her elbow. "But the lady won't be needing one." He pressed a bill into the man's hand. "For your trouble."

The driver glanced at it, his face suddenly wreathing with a smile. "Thank you, sir." And the money was quickly shoved into his pocket as he turned away.

Her lips moved to protest, but it was useless to openly oppose this man. At this point, it was better to accept his offer calmly than to make a fuss.

"I hope I won't be taking you out of your way, Mr. Riordan," Jill said as his hand guided her towards the parking lot.

"Not at all, Miss Randall." There was a suggestion of mockery in the deepening grooves around his mouth. "I had no particular destination in mind. I have a tendancy toward claustrophobia whenever I spend any time in town."

The car door was held open for her. Jill didn't coment until he had slid behind the wheel beside her. "You seem to fit in very well with the city environment." Her gaze wandered over the the perfectly tailored gray slacks and black blazer and the molding knit of his turtleneck sweater.

His gaze flickered to her briefly before he looked

over his shoulder to reverse out of the parking space. "Do you believe clothes make the man, Miss Randall?"

"Jill," she corrected absently, then answered his question. "You don't appear uncomfortable in them."

"That's strange . . . Jill." He hesitated deliberately over her Christian name, making it come out husky and mocking. "I would have thought you would realize that a wolf in sheep's clothing is still a wolf."

"Are you a wolf, Mr. Riordan?" Unwittingly her voice dropped the façade of innocence and became slightly baiting.

"Call me Riordan. I'm a lone wolf who prefers to travel without the supposed benefit of a pack or a mate."

Jill leaned back in her seat. Was he warning her? Did he think she was making a play for him? Surely not. She had not flirted with him once or given him a single indication that she was interested in him as anything more than Todd's brother and Kerry's future brother-in-law.

Maybe he had become accustomed to women pursuing him. A lot of women would be attracted to that dangerous air he possessed. Catching him would be a challenge. Under different circumstances, she might have tried herself, just for the fun of it.

"You can travel faster that way," she agreed. Directing her gaze out of the moving car window, she pretended an interest in the passing scenery. Silence seemed a way to end this vaguely personal conversation

"Are you from Montana?" Riordan didn't let the silence last for long.

"Yes. My parents live in West Yellowstone, where I was born and raised."

"You must be accustomed to spectacular scenery."

"Does anyone ever become accustomed to it? I hope not," Jill smiled naturally.

"Do you have any brothers or sisters?"

"Four. Three brothers and one sister."

"Older or younger than you?" Riordan asked, turning the wheel to guide the car around the corner.

"I have a brother who's two years older than me. The rest are younger." She darted a quick glance at his averted profile, curious why he was interested in her family background. A germ of an idea took root. "Andy, my older brother, is the only one of us who's married. He met his wife when he was stationed with the Marine Corps in California. He called my parents up one night and told them he was married. It was quite a shock for all of us, but once we had a chance to get to know his wife, Sally, we all liked her."

He turned his head slightly, running an eye over her face. "Subtlety is not one of your accomplishments, is it?" he suggested dryly.

"But I've never failed to be persevering," Jill returned with a malicious sparkle in her azure eyes.

"But your brother is your business and my brother is mine." The line of his mouth was inflexible, the firm set of his features yielding not one fraction to her honey-coated attempt at persuasion.

A thundering discovery vibrated over Jill with the suddenness of a summer storm. An intangible something had been troubling her ever since the first time she had seen Riordan, some little something that set him markedly apart from any man she had ever known. This very second she realized what it was.

Riordan didn't like her. Not because she was beautiful or because he believed she was dumb. It was because she was a woman. Jill held herself motionless, letting her mind register the discovery. Riordan was a woman hater. No, hate wasn't the right word. He viewed them with contempt, mocking the sentimental yearnings of their soul and using them to satisfy physical needs. But why?

His childhood couldn't have have been much different from Todd's, and Todd bore no emotional scars from the evident separation of their parents that Riordan had referred to briefly. Had he fallen in love with a woman at some time and been rejected?

It was possible, Jill conceded. He was a passionate man for all his impassive exterior. Not passionate in the erotic sense of the word, but in the depth of his convictions and feelings. He could carry a grudge for a very long time. Those gray eyes of his sliced through the fancy trappings of the modern world to leave only the basics. He wore the cloak of civilization when circumstances demanded, as now, but he was a man of the elements—primitive, ruthless, and strong.

So very opposite to Todd.

Jill brushed a hand in front of her eyes. Was this insight a blessing or a curse? She didn't want to know such things about Riordan. She didn't even want to think them.

Forcing her eyes to focus on the passing scenery, Jill willed her mind to concentrate on it. They had turned onto the main street of Helena called Last Chance Gulch.

Once it had been a gulch of the prickly pear and not a main paved street. That was in the beginning when four luckless prospectors had arrived to take their "last chance" at stricking it rich. That July of 1864, they found color in their gold pans and by autumn, a hundred makeshift cabins made up the goldrush settlement of Last Chance Gulch.

A town had been born. Last Chance Gulch was not a dignified name and survived only through the early months of the town's birth. Then the occupants changed it to Helena, naming the main street, where twenty million dollars in gold was mined, Last Chance Gulch.

The old, weathered buildings provided fertile colorful history for Jill to dwell on. The south end of Last Chance Gulch had been the sight of Chinatown. The Chinese, who had provided much of the labor to build the railroads, also cultivated truck gardens and operated their own stores. They even had a long tunnel beneath their particular section that they had used as a private opium den.

The architecture of the old buildings was predominantly Romanesque. Stone arches and columns combined with frieze and cornice and heavy timbers. The car was turning around another corner, leaving Last Chance Gulch to pass the Great Northern Depot which once, before the earthquake, possessed a tall clock tower. Then Jill's attention was caught by the Moorish style of the former Shrine Temple, now the Heléna Civic Center.

"What are you thinking about?" Riordan interrupted the silence again.

Jill could feel the cool touch of his eyes, but kept her gaze centered on the lighted street. "The city, its history," she shrugged.

A shiver danced over her skin as she wished she had never met him, or been momentarily entranced by his arrogant harshly handsome looks.

"Really?" was the aloofly disbelieving reply.

The car slowed to pull into the curb in front of the dormitory entrance. The engine was switched off and Riordan partially turned to face her. The metallic glitter of his gaze shimmered over the gold of Jill's hair, burnished by the outside streetlight.

His arm stretched negligently on the back of the seat, his hand only spare inches from her head. Jill tensed slightly, reacting to the latent animal instinct that warned her to tread lightly.

"I thought you might be thinking of some new tactic to maneuver me into changing my mind." His voice was low and cynical.

"Maneuver?" Jill swallowed. Her lashes fluttered, a gold brown fringe above deepening blue eyes.

"Isn't that what you've been doing since we met?" The softly dangerous tone dared her to deny it.

"I don't know what you mean," Jill protested weakly. Her facade as an ingenue was being stripped away by his slicing gaze and she was helpless to stop it. "If you mean, have I tried to convince you to give Kerry and Todd a chance? I have to admit that I have."

"Do you honestly expect me to believe you're as innocent as you appear?" Riordan smiled coldly, his amusement secret and at her expense.

"You're talking in circles." Jill fluttered her lashes in uncertain confusion, tossing her head to the side in bewilderment. "I don't understand what you're saying."

"Your act was very good, but intelligence has a way of letting itself be seen."

"My act?" she repeated blankly.

Inside she knew she couldn't admit that there was any truth to his accusations. If she stopped playing the "dumb blonde" now, she would end up losing her temper and telling him exactly what she thought of his arrogant ways. That anger would not help Kerry at all, although it would certainly release some of her own frustration.

"Really, Mr. Riordan, you just aren't making any sense." She reached for the door handle of the car. "I'd better be going inside."

It was locked. For a poised instant, her eyes searched frantically for the release before she realized that it was on the driver's side. Unwillingly she had to turn back to his mocking expression.

"Would you please unlock the door?"

Her request was met with silence and a complacent look. Jill nervously ran her tongue over her lower lip. The action focused his attention on her mouth.

"How do butterflies steal the nectar from so many flowers and remain looking untouched?" His own mouth twisted cynically, not requiring a reply.

Butterfly! The word shivered over her skin, goosebumps rising along the back of her neck. Only yesterday Jill had used that very word to describe herself. Riordan had chosen the same one. Coincidence? Or had some mysterious something passed between them, giving each the insight about the other?

"Why . . . why did you say butterfly?" She had to ask the question, her voice breathless and at odds with the guileless expression.

"Because," Riordan answered slowly and arrogantly, "you are as beautiful, as fragile, and about as constant as a butterfly." It was a condemnation, not a compliment. The back of a finger followed a strand of tawny gold hair brushed away from her face in its windblown style and down the back of her neck. Jill was pinned, like the butterfly he called her, by his steel-sharp gaze. "I've always wondered if the honey tastes sweeter fron the lips of a butterfly."

His hand cupped the back of her neck, fingers twisting into her hair, adding further pressure to draw Jill toward him. Her hands spread across his chest in resistance.

A soft, surprised, "No!" was offered in protest.

A tug of her hair turned her face up to meet his descending mouth, a flash of cynical amusement in its hard line an instant before it captured her lips.

Brutally harsh, he ravaged her mouth. There was a buzzing in her ears, hot fires of humiliation raced through her veins. In another second, Jill felt, surely her neck would break under the force of his kiss.

, It was not the way a man would kiss a woman but the way a man would take his pleasure of a tramp, without a thought or a care to her feelongs. But his strength was overpowering. Her struggles were only the useless flutterings of butterfly wings against iron bars.

Beneath her doubled fists straining against his chest, she could feel the steady beating of his heart. Her own was hammering like a mad thing. The bruising kiss was sapping all her strength, taking it from her as if it was nectar from a flower. She had to dredge the very depths of her reserves to keep from submitting weakly to his punishing embrace.

Riordan had attacked with the swiftness of an eagle swooping on its prey. With the same unexpectedness, he freed her mouth and relaxed the talon-hard grip on her neck, his fingers sliding to her fragile collarbone, capable of snapping it at the least provocation. Jill's head sank wearily in defeat, her tousled golden hair cascading forward over his hand to conceal the flaming humiliation in her cheeks.

But she wasn't allowed the precious seconds to regain her whirling equilibrium and take the calming breaths of air. Her chin was captured between his thumb and forefinger and raised so Riordan could inspect the extent of his conquest. Mirrored in his silver eyes was her own flushed and resentful expression, nothing more.

"Which of us is stronger, Miss Randall?" His lip curled in a derisive smile.

"Physically you are!" she hissed, blue flames shooting from her eyes, but Riordan was made of steel, not wood, and the fire harmlessly ricocheted over its target.

The grooves around his mouth deepened. "Don't make the mistake of thinking it's only physical," he warned in a low voice.

Releasing her completely, he was once again sitting behind the wheel. A movement of his hand near the control panel was followed by the comforting click of the car door being unlocked.

"Goodnight, Miss Randall."

Her knees trembled badly as she stepped from the car onto the curb. His assault on her—it could hardly be termed an embrace—had shaken her more than she realized, but it hadn't broken her spirit. With the security of distance between them, she turned, holding the door open as she leaned down to glare at him.

"Don't you make the mistake of thinking it's over, Riordan. I'm going to do everything I can to make certain Kerry and Todd are married as soon as possible!" She hurled the glove of challange, slammed the door and pivoted sharply toward the building.

For a few quaking steps, Jill thought he might come

after her. Unconsciously she held her breath, expelling it in a long sigh when she heard the snarl of the car engine. Those were bold words she had spoken, but she was determined to make them fact.

Kerry returned some time past midnight. Jill was in her single bed, feigning sleep. Her mind was too filled with vindictive thoughts. She doubted if she could hold them back in the intimacy of a late night chat, and it was better if Kerry never found out about what had happened. Fortunately no attempt was made to waken her as her dark-haired roommate changed into her nightclothes and slipped silently into the small bed opposite Jill's.

Morning brought the exhilarating knowledge that Riordan was on his way out of town if not already gone. Jill's sleep had been plagued by the lurking memory of his bruising kiss, but the rising sun seemed to burn away the humiliation she had suffered at his hands. Kerry, too, had seemed more relaxed and less haunted when she had dressed to meet Todd for church.

Arching her back, stretching cramping muscles, Jill couldn't help wondering what had taken place during Todd's meeting with Riordan that morning. Whatever had transpired, she could be sure of one thing—Riordan hadn't experienced a change of heart.

She blinked her eyes tiredly. Her mind was wandering from the task at hand again. If she had concentrated on what she was doing, the term paper would have been done an hour ago, she scolded herself, and forced her gaze to focus on the bonded paper in the typewriter.

As she removed the error-free sheet, the hallway door opened. Jill glanced around to identify Kerry entering the room.

"Excellent timing, Kerry," she greeted her room-mate with a smiling sigh. "This is the last page. The typewriters is all yours."

"I brought you a sandwich and a Coke. I thought you'd probably be hungry." Kerry motioned toward the paper bag she had set on the bureau top.

"You're a lifesaver!" Jill gathered up her papers and stacked them on the corduroy quilted cover of her bed. With the bag in hand, she returned to the bed, curling her long legs beneath her to sit cross-legged near the head of the bed. "You and Todd must have gone out to dinner after church."

Her comment was met with silence. A curious frown pulled Jill's arched brows together as she glanced up. Kerry was going through the motions of hanging her dusty-rose coat in the closet, but her mind seemed far removed from the task.

"Kerry?" Jill snapped her fingers to prod her friend back to the present.

"What?" Kerry looked around blankly. "I'm sorry. Did you say something?"

"Nothing important." Jill set the Coke on the table between the two beds and took the wrapped sandwich from the bag. "You were in a daze."

"Was I?" The coat was carefully hung in the closet before Kerry walked slowly to her bed. She sat on the edge, staring thoughtfully at the hands she clasped in her lap. "I suppose I was thinking," she murmured.

"That's a safe guess," Jill teased, but her expression was marked with concern. "Of course, the next question is what were you thinking about?"

The hands twisted nervously in her lap. "You remember that Todd met with Riordan this morning."

"Yes." Her blue gaze hardened warily. She unwrapped the sandwich, pretending an interest in it. "What did the great man have to say?" She couldn't keep the sarcasm out of her voice.

"Todd's application for a transfer to Harvard has been accepted. Riordan received the notification at the ranch this last week," Kerry told her.

So Riordan had another ace up his sleeve, Jill thought angrily. All he had to do was keep Todd and Kerry apart for the summer and the distance between Montana and the East Coast would take care of the rest of the year. He was probably counting on out of sight being out of mind.

"You and Todd will have to set the wedding date for some time in August, then, won't you?" Jill tossed her head back, letting the shaggy, golden curls trail down her back. "With your grade point you could easily transfer to a university out there."

"I couldn't afford the out-of-state tuition, though," Kerry sighed.

As Riordan had no doubt guessed, Jill added savagely to herself. "And Todd wouldn't be able to help because Riordan is still holding the threat of shutting off the money supply over his head." Her fingers tightened on the sandwich, smashing the bread and wishing it was Riordan's neck. "The two of you can't allow him to blackmail you this way!"

"Todd doesn't think we should do anything too hasty yet."

"He surely doesn't think Riordan is going to change his mind. This isn't the age of miracles." At the pinched lines that appeared around Kerry's mouth, Jill wished the her reply hadn't been so completely negative. She should have left her friend with a little hope.

"Well," Kerry breathed in deeply, "Riordan did make a proposition to Todd this morning."

"What kind?" Jill was skeptical of any proposition Riordan would offer.

"He . . . he conceded that he might have been too harsh and quick in his judgement."

"That's big of him," Jill grumbled, biting into her sandwich.

"He admits he was prejudiced against me before we ever met and that he should at least get to know me better. He still doesn't approve of the engagement," Kerry hastened to add.

"So what has he suggested?" Jill asked dryly. "A trial period?"

Unitl the autumn term started and Todd was gone to Harvard, Jill completed the thought silently.

"Something like that," her roommate admitted, finally lifting her gaze from the twining fingers in her lap to look at Jill. "Todd works at the ranch in the summer. Riordan has invited me to spend a month there so he and I can get better acquainted."

Total disaster, was Jill's first thought. Kerry was already intimidated by the man. A month in his company would totally subdue her even with Todd's support. Jill did not underestimate Riordan. She knew his capabilities and the lengths he would go to achieve his ends.

She stared at her sandwich. "There is an obstacle to his invitation, Kerry. How are you going to stay at his ranch and earn money to pay for your fall term as well?" Both she and Kerry were going to work for Jill's parents that summer in their motel restaurant near the entrance to Yellowstone Park. "Mom and dad will have to hire someone to take your place. You won't even have a summer job after you've spent a month there."

"Riordan has offered to compensate me for that."

She should have guessed he would cover every contingency. Jill stuffed the partially eaten sandwich back in the sack. It had begun to taste like cotton.

"You can't seriously be considering the offer," Jill protested desperately, pressing two fingers against her forehead, trying to rub away the throbbing ache that had started between her eyes. "You know it wouldn't work. He'd make your life a total misery. You know what he can be like when Todd isn't around. How long do you think you could take it?"

"I couldn't, not alone. But—" thin brown eyes became round and pleading, engulfing the plainly petite features in a lost helpless look— "if you were with me—"

"I'll let you in on a little secret," Jill interrupted quickly, drawing a deep breath and untangling her legs. "Riordan doesn't like me and he isn't about to invite me to spend a month at his ranch. Besides I, too, have to work this summer."

"Jill." Something in Kerry's voice put her instantly on guard. "Riordan thought it might not look right for me to stay there at the house for a month with Todd and him. I mean, he does have a housekeeper, but . . . well, he invited you to come, too, as a kind of chaperone—with the same offer of compensation."

"Oh, no!" Jill was on her feet, striding away from the bed to the solitary window. Sunlight glistened platinum gold over her hair dancing around her shoulders as she shook her head vigorously. Her hands rubbed the chilling gooseflesh on her upper arms. "No!"

"Please." There was a throbbing ache in the coaxing tone.

Jill spun around. "It just wouldn't work, Kerry."

Lord, but that man had a devious mind! He had considered every possible argument she could have made to prevent Kerry from going.

That he had invited Jill confirmed the magnitude of his arrogance. She had challenged him and now he was offering a front row seat for her to watch him tear the engagement apart. Riordan would have his revenge and be aware of any move Jill made to thwart

his attempts. Jill had underestimated him again, and
she didn't like the sensation of being bested.

Kerry's soulful eyes didn't see any of that. "You
must come."

"Don't you see," Jill protested in agitation, "if I
come I'll end up losing my temper and only make the
situation worse for you and Todd. The wisest thing for
you to do is refuse the invitation and take the chance
that Riordan won't be able to influence Todd into
breaking the engagement. That's the most logical
thing, because Todd does love you."

"I can't."

The dark head was turned away, tears misting
diamond bright in her brown eyes. Jill wanted to take
her by the shoulders and shake her hard.

"Why can't you? You can't go there alone!"

"Yes, I can." Kerry brushed away a tear with her
hand and let her unreproachful gaze meet Jill's impatient look. "I love Todd. I don't want to come between
him and his brother. Not having a family I think I
know how important it is. If there's only the slimmest
chance that Riordan might approve of Todd marrying me after spending a month at the ranch, I'll take it.
I'd feel better if you would come with me, but I'm
going either way."

"Kerry, this is a stupid time to turn heroic," Jill
sighed. Her mouth thinned in self-anger at the way
Kerry winced from the unconsciously cutting remark
against her natural timidity. "Besides, there're my
parents to consider. They're expecting me to work this
summer, not have a vacation. I couldn't tell them at

the last minute that they're going to have to find someone else to take my place."

"You said yourself that they have more applications than jobs. They could easily hire someone else," Kerry reminded her quietly.

"I suppose they could," Jill conceded grudgingly, "but they would never agree to this plan. Riordan has a housekeeper. You said so yourself, and chaperones went out of fashion with hoop skirts."

"You could call them and see."

Staring into the resigned yet pleading face of her roommate, Jill knew she would have to make the telephone call. What kind of a friend would she be if she let this poor defenseless creature walk into Riordan's lion den without protection? The question was, who was going to protect Jill? She hoped her parents would.

They were infuriatingly understanding.

CHAPTER FOUR

THE BIG SKY COUNTRY. The last of the big-time spenders. That's the way the brochures described Montana. The vast prairielands in the east rolled westward, gathering speed to swell into mountains towering like a tidal wave over the landscape.

Looking over the horizon where majestic mountain peaks tried to pierce the crystal blue bubble of sky, Jill felt the answering surge of her heartbeat. Their early summer coat of vivid green could only be rivalled by the bold splash of autumn or the stark white purity of winter.

Now it was green, a multitude of shades broken only by the dark brown of tree trunks driving upward toward the sky, the rocky faces of the mountains catching the golden sun, and the gay pinks, yellows and white of wild flowers dotting the meadows and craggy slopes. Breathtaking and awesome, the scenery remained constant while ever-changing. The tremendous sensation of being released from an earthbound existence to soar to some magnificent plateau was overwhelming.

"I feel it every time," Jill murmured.

"What did you say?" Kerry glanced at her curiously, not quite catching the softly spoken words.

"I was admiring the scenery." Reluctantly she drew her gaze to the interior of the car. "I never tire of looking at the mountains, especially when you can see them like this, unbroken by any man-made structure."

"They make me feel small and insignificant," Kerry inserted, "but they are beautiful."

Jill leaned forward to glance around her friend at their driver. "I've lived in Montana all my life, but always in town. What's it like, Todd, to live in the mountains year round?"

He smiled faintly sliding a brief look to her. "I don't know."

What?" Her blond head tilted to the side in surprise.

"When I was born my mother moved into town. I only spent the summers with my father on the ranch," he explained. "So I have no idea what it's like to be in the country during the last days of Indian summer or see the first winter storm clouds building on the mountain peaks. I've often wondered, too, what it would be like, but never enough to find out."

"I didn't know. I mean, Kerry did mention that your parents didn't live together, but I guess I assumed they didn't separate until you were older." Jill leaned back, staring thoughtfully ahead. It was difficult to imagine Riordan growing up in a town. The image of him being raised in the mountains under the domination of the elements was much easier to accept.

"Of course, Riordan was older than you. The adjustment must have been harder for him."

"He wouldn't try to adjust," Todd replied. "My mother told me that the minute he found out that she wasn't ever going back to the ranch, he ran away. He was nine years old and hitchhiked all the way back to the ranch. That happened three or four times before my grandfather suggested that it might be better to let Riordan stay on the ranch with his father. She finally agreed. When I was older I remembered asking him one time how he'd had the courage to come all the way from Helena, where mom and I lived with her father, to the ranch by himself." The corners of his mouth were turned up in a wry smile. "He said there wasn't any other way he could get home. The ranch has always been home to him. For me, it's just a place to spend the summer vacation."

There was a twinge of envy that Riordan could rightfully call the mountains home. Then Jill considered the singleminded determination of the nine-year-old boy who had traveled the hundred and fifty-odd miles southwest of Helena.

That part of him hadn't changed. Now he was determined to prevent a marriage between Todd and Kerry. He wasn't going to let anything stand in his way. He had even invited Jill along to watch.

Drawing in a deep breath, Jill moved her head slightly in angry despair. There were three fools in this car. She wasn't sure which of them was the biggest. Probably herself, since the other two were blinded by their love for each other. The month promised to be a long and trying one—if she and Kerry survived.

"What was Riordan like as a boy?" It was better to find out as much as she could about the enemy.

"I don't know," Todd answered thoughtfully. "When you're a kid yourself, you don't pay much attention to those things. He was always 'big brother,' teaching me to ride, taking me hunting, letting me tag along. He was just Riordan."

Kerry shuddered involuntarily. Todd reached out and covered the small hand on her knee with his own. Out of the corner of her eye, Jill saw the reassuring squeeze.

"Don't start worrying," he murmured softly. "Once he gets to know you, he'll see what a great sister you'll make."

Jill fell silent. Todd seemed unable to tell her much about Riordan and the mention of his name was only making Kerry more uneasy. A smile tugged at the corners of her mouth. She was concerned about making Kerry uneasy, when she had been sitting on pins and needles for the last half hour herself. The points had grown sharper as they came closer to their destination. It couldn't be far now. They had turned off the main highway several miles back.

As if on cue Todd slowed the car and turned on to a dirt road leading farther into the mountain wilderness. The fence opening had no gate as the tires thumped over a cattle guard.

"This is it," he announced, nodding his head at the

window to indicate the land around them. "The house is a few miles back."

Glancing back, Jill couldn't see any sign identifying the ranch as Riordan's property. The only sign she had noticed was one saying: No Tresspassing. A prophetic warning, perhaps?

A midafternoon sun glittered in her eyes as they topped a meadow rise and Jill caught her first glimpse of the ranch house. Large evergreens stood in a horseshoe guard on three sides of the house, protecting it from sweeping winter winds. The two-storied house itself was a tasteful example of turn-of-the century architecture, with its entrance porch a columned portico. Yet its wood and stone exterior was in keeping with its rustic setting.

"It's beautiful!" Kerry breathed, breaking the spell of immobility after the car had stopped in front.

"Just a little cabin in the mountians," Todd jested, opening his door and stepping out.

It wasn't a mansion, but its graceful, old-world lines were impressive just the same, Jill decided. Curiosity burned to see the inside.

As she stepped out of the car, her gaze swept to the ranch buildings. There was no sign of any activity either there or in the house. She had expected Riordan to be on hand to greet them, subconsciously she was braced to meet his cynical, mocking gray eyes.

"I didn't expect it to be so nice," Kerry whispered.

Jill glanced at the petite brunette now standing beside her. "I for one can hardly wait to see if the inside lives up to the promise of the outside," she replied quietly, turning to walk to the rear of the car where Todd was unloading their luggage.

With Todd carrying the heavier cases and the two girls the lightweight ones, they mounted the steps to the heavy oak door.

The formal entry hall gleamed with hardwood wainscoting below bright upper walls of cream yellow. A carved oak staircase led to the upper floor at the end of the hall. On their left was a fireplace of native granite, the trophy head of a big sheep hanging above the mantel. The hardwood floor beneath their feet was inlaid geometric designs, known as parquetry.

Todd set the cases onto the floor. "I wonder where Mary is," he frowned.

Footsteps approached, unhurried and light. Jill's head turned in their direction, wondering what kind of a woman this Mary was. Anyone who kept house for Riordan would have to be a paragon of talents to satisfy him. From the polished entrance hall, Jill guessed that the housekeeper was.

If there had been a subconscious image of the housekeeper, Jill wasn't aware of it. Yet astonishment crackled through her at the sight of the young, almond-eyed woman who came into view.

Long chestnut hair flowed around her shoulders as the sensuously curved woman glided toward them. Her eyes were a tawny hazel shade like a cat's and there was a purring quality about her smile.

"Welcome home, Todd." She ignored both girls to

walk directly to Todd and press a less-than-motherly kiss on his cheek.

Jill doubted if the woman was Riordan's age, although her bone structure was deceiving and it was possible she was in her very early thirties. It wasn't difficult for Jill to believe that her talents went beyond housekeeping.

Todd laughed self-consciously and glanced at Kerry before returning his attention to the woman whose hand was still resting lightly on his arm. "I didn't expect to see you here, Sheena."

Sheena? This wasn't Mary, the housekeeper? Jill's eyebrows lifted fractionally in further surprise. The woman was certainly acting the hostess and not a guest.

The purring smile deepened although it didn't reach the woman's cat-gold eyes. "I've been deputized as your official welcoming committee. Riordan had to be away from the ranchyard this afternoon. I'm sorry I didn't hear you drive in, but I was in the kitchen helping Mary with dinner tonight."

"I . . . I hope you're joining us," Todd offered politely but with little enthusiasm.

"I am." Then the woman's gaze swung to Jill, indifferent in its appraisal of her blond hair and blue eyes. "I'm Sheena Benton, Riordan's closest neighbor. You must be Todd's girlfriend. Kerry, isn't it?"

Closest neighbor? Is that all? Jill thought cynically as she smoothly shook the artistically long and slender hand offered to her.

"No, I'm Jillian Randall, Kerry's friend," she corrected lightly.

The tawny eyes narrowed fleetingly before they darted to the plain, dark-haired girl at Jill's side. An uncomfortable flush in Kerry's cheeks indicated her painful awareness of Jill's obvious beauty, her golden looks intensified by Kerry's mouse-soft coloring.

Jill wanted to cry out at the faint condemnation in the woman's eyes. Kerry's beauty was on the inside, but Jill doubted if this feline creature would understand.

Sheena Benton laughed throatily at her own mistake. There wasn't any amusement, however, when the tawny gaze refocused on Jill. There was a glitter of malevolence in the almond-shaped eyes. Instinctively Jill glanced at the woman's hands, half expecting to see them transformed into cat's claws to scratch her face.

"It's a pleasure to meet you, Jillian," Sheena declared in a husky voice. Liar, Jill thought to herself. "I must admit you hardly look like a chaperone."

"I'm really here as Kerry's friend."

Her hand was released as the woman turned to Kerry and inclined her head in a falsely apologetic fashion. "I'm sorry about the mistake," Sheena Benton said in a regal tone.

"It's quite all right," Jill murmured self-consciously.

Kerry glanced through the corner of her lashes at Todd as though fearful he might suddenly be seeing how plain and unobtrusive she was. Warm, hazel eyes affectionately returned her surreptitious look.

"You'll probably be very grateful for your friend's company after you've been here awhile," Sheena continued. "At the end of a week, the magnificent scenery around here begins to pale when you have nothing else to do. That's when boredom sets in."

"You don't look bored, Miss Benton," Jill couldn't resist inserting.

"But then I live here. I've had a few town friends stay with me. Invariably they begin climbing the walls after a week." A cold smile was directed at Jill. "And it's Mrs. Benton."

"You're married?" she returned with some surprise.

"Widowed," was the complacent reply. "My husband was killed in a hunting accident four years ago."

"It must have been a shock," Jill suggested dryly.

"In the beginning I was kept much too busy trying to keep the ranch going, and by the time Riordan helped me find a competent manager, the worst of the shock had passed." Feline shoulders shrugged as if to say the marriage was long ago and forgotten. "As the owner, I still have enough responsibilities to keep me occupied. I don't have time to be bored."

"Neither will Kerry," Todd grinned, indifferent to the invisible sparks flying between Sheena and Jill. "I intend to devote every spare moment to making sure she enjoys this month."

"Spoken like a typical young lover," Sheena laughed throatily, mocking their youth. "You'll find life operates at a simpler level, Kerry. A night out will probably consist of a walk in the moonlight. Todd is a patient teacher, though. Maybe in a month you'll be a country girl like me."

"Not too much of a country girl," Todd qualified Sheena's statement. "We're going to be living most of our life in cities. I want to keep Kerry mainly a town bird."

The light shining in Kerry's eyes said she would be whatever Todd wanted her to be. In that silent second, Jill forgot the chestnut-haired woman with the tawny eyes and remembered the reason she was in this house. Her mission was to do everything in her power to make certain Kerry and Todd lived happily ever after, as the fairy tales put it.

"Let me show you two girls to your rooms," Sheena inserted smoothly, turning towards the staircase at the end of the entrance hall. "I know you'll want to unpack and bathe and rest before dinner. Naturally you have your old room, Todd," she tossed over her shoulder.

Jill and Kerry followed the woman gliding effortlessly over the flowered carpet that covered the stairs. Sheena Benton seemed intent on impressing them with the idea that she was the hostess in the house, and not just for the afternoon.

"I hope you girls don't mind sharing a bathroom." Sheena paused at the top of the stairs for them to catch up. "You have adjoining rooms with a bathroom in between."

"Sounds fine," Jill nodded.

"Good." With a brief smile, the woman walked familiarly down the wainscoted hallway, opened a door and stepped to the side. "This is your room, Kerry."

There was a fleeting impression of delicate shades of green before the petite brunette moved hesitantly into the doorway to block Jill's view. Sheena was already pivoting away, indicating that Jill follow her.

"And your room, Jillian, is here," she said.

The door swung open to a room dominated by white with a sprinkling of blue, contrasted by artistically carved woodwork of glistening walnut. A Persian rug in an intricate design of blue and white covered the floor. The skillfully styled furniture in the room was, if Jill didn't miss her guess, antique.

Her eyes sparkled with appreciation and admiration as she stepped farther into the room. The large double bed had a white cover hand-crocheted in a popcorn stitch—the perfect touch.

Setting her small suitcases on the floor, Jill turned to the woman standing in the doorway. "It's lovely," she murmured inadequately.

Any further attempt to express her delight with the room was checked by the look in Sheena's face. It forcibly said not to become too enamored of a room she would only have for a month. Then Sheena's eyes seemed to change from an amber warning shade to an aloof tawny gold.

"The bathroom and your friend's room are through there," she said, flicking a hand toward the door near the fireplace. "Dinner is at seven."

"Thank you."

But Jill's polite words were spoken to a closing door. She pursed her lips thoughtfully. Something told her she had to watch out not only for Riordan but for Sheena as well. The woman didn't like her or want her here.

Shaking her head to rid her mind of its unwelcome thoughts, Jill walked to the connecting door. The bathroom was large and spacious, its fixtures old-fashioned but seemingly in working condition. The murmur of Todd's and Kerry's voices in the adjoining room made Jill tap discreetly on the door to her friend's bedroom.

"Come in," Todd called.

A flushed Kerry was trying to squirm out of his arms when Jill walked into the room, but he wouldn't let her go, taking delight in her shyness.

"I did knock," Jill pointed out with a teasing smile.

"Todd, please!"

"Oh, all right," he laughed down at Kerry. Partially releasing her with one hand, he captured her chin and dropped a quick kiss on the button nose. Only then did he let Kerry go and turned to pick up the large blue suitcase belonging to Jill.

"I'll carry this into your room. By the way—" Todd paused after taking two steps "—what did you think of Tiger-eyes, Jill?"

Grimancing wryly, she shrugged. "I didn't realize it was possible to dislike someone on sight."

"Sheena has staked a claim on Riordan. She

doesn't like it when anyone gets too near, especially when they look like you."

"Your warning is duly noted, but she hasn't got anything to worry about from me. I'm not interested in her claim," Jill declared. "She's welcome to Riordan. They would make a perfect pair."

"Please, it's bad enough having her as a neighbor," Todd's brow arched expressively. "Don't wish her on me as a sister-in-law!"

"Todd, you shouldn't say things like that," Kerry protested gently. Love filled his face with a tender smile when he glanced at her. "Why? Because I prefer my women feminine instead of feline?" he teased.

"Go and take Jill's suitcase into her room." Despite the ordering tone, Jill could see the glow lighting Kerry's face at Todd's compliment. She very nearly looked beautiful.

"Whatever you say," he winked, and this time made it out of the room.

Kerry stared after him for a moment. Wrapping her arms around herself as if to ward off a sudden chill, she looked away from Jill's inquiring look.

"Well, we're here," she sighed.

"It's a fabulous place, isn't it?" Jill replied to avoid any discussion of the reason they were here.

Brown eyes swung admiringly around the room. "Todd told me about it, but I didn't expect anything like this. His grandfather built the house for his wife. Can you imagine how difficult it was back then? All the furniture was shipped by rail to Bannack, then by wagon here."

Jill wandered over to the four-poster bed with its canopy of spring green. Her hand trailed over the quilted cover on the bed. Varying shades of pale green material had been painstakingly stitched together in an intricate geometric pattern joined against a background of almost white green.

"This is beautiful. The one in my room is crocheted. Whoever did these had to have a lot of patience."

"A lot of love," Kerry corrected softly. "It's these little touches that keep the place from seeming like a museum. It's a home because someone cared about the people in it. She took the time to make these because she cared and because she was proud of the home where she lived. Oh, Jill—" her voice trembled with emotion "—I can hardly wait until I can have a home of my own. Some women are made to have a careers, but I'm not. I want a husband and children and a place where I can do things like this for them."

"You will," Jill promised lightly. "In the meantime, I suppose we should start getting unpacked. I want to take a bath and change clothes before dinner. Sheena said it was at seven."

Kerry glanced at the slender watch on her wrist. "It's later than I thought. We'll have just about enough time to make it."

"That's probably just as well. I had the feeling Sheena didn't want us sticking our noses outside the door until then." The edges of her mouth turned up in wry amusement as she moved away from the bed toward the connecting door. "I'll leave you to unpack. Whoever gets done first takes the first bath."

"It's a deal," the other girl agreed.

Jill was the first to finish unpacking and lazed in the luxuriously deep tub until Kerry was done. In her bedroom, she slid a lace-trimmed slip over her undergarments and walked to the small vanity table. Her tawny gold hair was piled on top of her head, held in place by a tortoiseshell clasp. Releasing the clasp, she shook her hair free with her fingers and reached for the hairbrush on the table.

Refreshed and stimulated by the relaxing bath, she wandered about the room. Her silken blond hair crackled with electricity from the rhythmic and vigourous strokes of the brush. Pausing near the panelled drapes of Prussian blue, she gazed through the lace insets. The window looked out of the rear of the house, giving her a breathtaking view of the mountains rising above the valley meadow of the ranch.

The sun had begun its descent in the vividly blue sky. The jutting mountains caught the golden fire, tranformed the rocky peaks into regal crowns. The strokes of the hairbrush slowed to a complete stop as Jill lifted aside the white lace curtains for an unobstructed view.

Deep green forests blanketed the mountain slopes in a thick velvet cape. She felt the witchery of the mountains reach out and capture her in its spell.

A movement in the long shadows of the guardian pines near the house caught the corner of her eye. Reluctantly, she let her gaze leave the majesty of the sun-bathed peaks. The outer ranch buildings were out of her sight beyond the stand of windbreak trees.

It was from that direction the tall figure had come, only now emerging from the shadows into the afternoon sunlight. Long reaching strides carried Riordan swiftly toward the rear of the house.

He was dressed as she had first seen him, in snug-fitting faded demins, a white shirt, dusty now, accenting his muscular chest, and cowboy boots, the sunlight catching the shiny glint of a spur.

One leather glove was off and he was pulling impatiently at the other. It was nearly off when Riordan stopped, halting fluidly almost in midstride. The jet-dark head raised, tipped slightly to the side as his gaze focused unswervingly on the window where Jill stood.

Startled, she started to step back, then realized he couldn't possibly see her at that angle and distance. The glove was slowly removed and folded in the other hand with its mate. Riordan's mouth quirked at the corner as he continued to stare at the window.

A blush of self-anger at her own stupidity roughed her cheeks. He couldn't see her, but he could see the curtain lifted aside. This was his home. He knew which room the window belonged to and he undoubtedly knew which room had been given to Jill.

Hastily she released the curtain and saw the amused upward curl of his mouth deepen. Then he was striding toward the house again, the leather gloves tapping the side of his leg in satifaction.

Irritated by her own schoolgirlish reaction, Jill

pivoted impatiently away from the window. She should have outstared him. She couldn't afford to let him have the slightest edge in any meeting. She wouldn't back down again.

"What are you wearing, Jill?" Kerry was standing in the open doorway of the bathroom, concentrating on tying the sash of her robe, so she missed the look of anger on her friend's face.

"The, er, rose crêpe," Jill replied, breathing in deeply to chase away any traces of temper. "It's summerish but not too dressy."

"I thought I'd wear my yellow flowered dress. What do you think?"

"It would be perfect." Her smile was taut and unnatural, but Kerry didn't notice it.

"I'll go and get dressed. Come into my room whenever you're ready," she announced, and turned toward her own room.

Jill walked to the walnut vanity mirror above the table. A few expert flicks of the brush achieved the windswept style of her hair, tousled like a wispy cloud trailing away from her face in shimmering waves of dusty amber. The pale tan of her complexion needed no makeup, a moisturizing cream provided a subdued glow. A very light application of eye shadow gave a hint of blue to intensify the color of her eyes.

"Applying warpaint," her reflection teased wickedly. Yes, Jill smiled, reaching for the mascara.

At half-past-six, she was ready and helping Kerry with the stubborn zipper of her dress.

"Do you think we should go down now? It isn't

seven yet,'' Kerry asked, standing quietly while Jill hooked the fastener.

"I don't see why not. It'll give us time to see more of the house before dinner.''

Kerry hesitated as Jill walked to the hall door. "Do I look all right?''

"Like a mountain flower,'' she grinned in a light-hearted response to ease her friend's attack of nerves. "Come on!''

They were three steps into the hallway leading to the stairs when Jill heard the approach of footsteps behind them, and her muscles stiffened automatically. It had to be Riordan. She hadn't heard him pass her room, but with his cat-soft way of walking, it was possible she wouldn't. Besides, it was only logical to assume he would shower and change after working all day.

The desire was there to pretend she didn't hear the firm strides of the man walking behind them. She might have ignored them if she hadn't seen Kerry glancing over her shoulder. There was no choice except for Jill to do the same.

No silver gray eyes met the sparkling challenge of hers. Instead she saw the darker softness of Todd's gazing warmly at the now halted Kerry. Relief shuddered through her. It wasn't a welcome reaction. She wanted to be more poised and in command than this when she met Riordan face to face.

Todd's hands were reaching out for Kerry's "You look beautiful, honey.''

"Do you think so?'' She gazed rapturously into his

eyes. The radiant glow of love chased away all her plainness, making her as beautiful as Todd declared she was.

Feeling superfluous, Jill said, "I'll see you two downstairs."

Ostensibly her presence in the house was as a chaperone and campanion to Kerry, but Jill didn't intend to turn into her friend's shadow. She and Todd were entitled to be alone once in a while, and Jill was going to make sure it was often.

At the base of the stairs, Jill hesitated. Glancing to the rear of the carved banister, she caught a glimpse of white-covered table through an open door. Guessing it was the dining room, she walked toward it.

The open door ahead of it led into the living room. She gave it a cursory glance of identification as she walked by, believing she was more likely to find her hostess in the dining room.

The oval table, covered by an intricately crocheted cloth, was set with fragile, flowered china and gleaming crystal. A chandelier hung from the crossbeamed ceiling to illuminate the table. A silken fabric covered the walls above the wainscoting, its white-on-white design alleviating the heavy darkness of the furniture and panelling. But the room was empty and Jill was not inclined to wait in there for the others.

Retracing her steps, she wandered into living room. Her gaze was drawn immediately to the painting hanging above the mantel of the marble-faced fireplace.

It was a portrait of a woman, a very beautiful

woman with copper hair and sparkling hazel eyes. The peach-tinted lips were curved in a breathless smile that embraced life. Yet, despite all the vitality flowing in every slender line, there was a definite air of fragility and innocence.

"My mother," a male voice said.

Jill whirled away from the portrait, to face the corner of the room from which Riordan's voice had come. Gray eyes mocked the wary look in her expression as he rose from a wing-backed chair, a glass in one hand.

He had changed from the dusty demins to tailored slacks of camel tan. The long-sleeved silk shirt, predominantly white with a design in green and tan, molded the breadth of his shoulders and tapered to his comparatively slim waist. The top buttons were undone, revealing dark, curling hairs on his chest. The black thickness of his hair glistened as if still damp from a shower.

Her rapid noting of his dress was being echoed by Riordan, although his slow appraisal of her was more insolent as he inspected the way the clinging material of her loose-fitting dress revealed her full curves without being blatantly suggestive.

His aloof gaze was stripping. Jill felt the heat of betrayal warming her face. But she refused to look away even when his mocking eyes stopped at her mouth, as if reminding her of the time he had punishingly possessed her lips.

"I've heard of pink elephants, Miss Randall, but pink butterflies?" His mouth quirked with cynical amusement. Unwillingly Jill protectivley touched the rose-colored material of her dress. "Would you like a drink?"

"No," she snapped, and regretted her sharpness as a dark brow raised suggestively in her direction. She added more quietly, "Thank you anyway."

It wouldn't do to lose her temper so early in the evening, and on her first night in his house, too.

"I must apologize for not being here to greet you and Miss Adams." His low derisive voice was not the least bit apologetic. "I hope you weren't at your window watching for me any extended length of time."

"I wasn't watching for *you*," Jill declared coldly. "I was enjoying the view of the mountains from my window."

Satisfaction glittered in his eyes. He had deliberately trapped her into admitting she had seen him and she had foolishly risen to the bait. She turned away, angry with herself for not being better prepared for this encounter.

An older woman was pausing in the doorway, wearing a dress of blue gingham with an apron in a matching blue tied around her large-boned frame. Short blue black hair was dulled by a suggestion of gray, but nothing dimmed the alertness of her nearly black eyes shining out of a strongly structured face as she glanced from Jill to Riordan. This was obviously the housekeeper, Jill decided.

"Mrs. Benton sent me in with this tray of nuts and olives," the woman explained, walking into the room.

"She said you'd be having drinks in here before coming to the table."

"Miss Randall, this is my housekeeper, Mary Rivers," Riordan confirmed Jill's deduction. "She's a full-blooded Crow Indian, the granddaughter of a war-chief. This is Jill Randall, a friend of the young lady Todd brought home."

"I'm pleased to meet you." Jill's smile came naturally, prompted by the friendliness in the woman's expression.

An answering smile crinkled the corners of the intelligent dark eyes. The lines had become ingrained from much use.

"I hope you enjoy your stay here, Miss Randall." The words of welcome were spoken sincerely—the first Jill had heard. "Despite my ancestry, I seldom go on the warpath! After thirty years in this house, it takes a lot to provoke me."

Jill darted a swift glance at Riordan's impassive face. Mary Rivers had obviously overheard his needling remarks and had offered a discreet word of advice—a suggestion easier said than done.

"May I help you with anything in the kitchen?" Jill offered.

"It's nearly all ready," the woman refused, still maintaining her warm smile. "And besides, too many cooks . . . ."

Her voice trailed away, leaving Jill with the impression that the housekeeper believed Sheena Benton already made it one-too-many cooks. The thought brought a smile she was forced to hide as the chestnut-

haired woman entered the room, bestowing a dazzling smile on Riordan.

"I'd best get back to the kitchen," the housekeeper
murmured, and withdrew.

The cat-flecked eyes of Sheena Benton weren't
quite so warm as they blinked at Jill. "Have you been
down long, Miss Randall? I'm afraid I was in the
kitchen."

"Only a few minutes," Jill acknowledged. Silently
and partly grudgingly, she admired the gold dress that
matched the woman's eyes and sensuously hugged her
curves.

Riordan's eyes were watching her above the rim of
the glass he held to his mouth. He probably knew his
tiger mistress did not like pink butterflies, either, and
was waiting for an excuse to claw the fragile wings.

When his gaze slid to the doorway, Jill followed it,
seeing Todd return a lipstick-stained handkerchief to
his pocket as he ushered a flushed and radiant Kerry
into the room.

CHAPTER FIVE

THE ODD NUMBER of people had placed Jill alone on one side of the oval table opposite Todd and Kerry with Riordan and Sheena as host and hostess at the ends of the table. Sheena had dominated the conversation with witty anecdotes of ranch life.

In the main, she had related stories that involved either Riordan or Todd, always subtly pointing out her closeness to the host and silently reminding Jill and Kerry that they were outsiders—Jill more so than Kerry.

Jill's ostracism hadn't ended in the dining room. She should have known Sheena couldn't have cut her out of the group without Riordan's approval. In the living room, Sheena as acting hostess naturally sat on the sofa in front of the silver coffee service and Riordan joined her.

Todd and Kerry took the two chairs opposite the sofa, which left Jill with only two choices. One was out of the question since it meant sitting on the sofa beside Riordan. Accepting the china cup and saucer from Sheena, Jill sat in the chair which placed her outside their circle.

Seething inwardly, Jill maintained an outward air

of calm and composure. She was not going to try to force her way into the conversation or draw attention to herself in any way. It would be what Riordan expected her to do. Instead she sat in apparent acceptance of her exile from the group and listened.

There was satisfaction in discovering that Kerry was no longer being excluded as Sheena offered a series of polite questions about her childhood, college life and studies. Kerry's replies were soft as they always were with strangers, but she answered without hesitation, a fact that Jill silently applauded, knowing the courage it required from her shy friend.

"Todd, you'll have to show Kerry the beaver pool," Sheena declared, glancing at the brunette after she had given the command. "It isn't far from the house, a nice walk and it's a perfect swimming pool. The water is a bit chilly since it's snow drainage from the mountains, but the setting is idyllic. It'll be something for you to do while Todd is working. You do swim, don't you?"

"Well, actually, I don't know how," Kerry replied self-consciously. "I never had the opportunity to learn while I was growing up."

"What about horseback riding? I'm sure Riordan could find you a suitably gentle mount. You'll enjoy an afternoon canter over the open meadow—that is, if you ride?" A feline brow arched inquiringly.

A hand nervously crept to a dark curl as Kerry darted a sideways glace at Todd. "I have ridden a couple of times, but I'm not very good."

Sheena smiled faintly. At Jill's angle she couldn't

tell if the smile was motivated by satisfaction or polite understanding. The latter seemed very unlikely. Riordan was leaning against the sofa back, apparently content to let Sheena suggest activities to occupy the free daylight hours.

"In any event—" Sheena shrugged away Kerry's lack of enthusiasm for horseback riding "—I know there'll be times when you'll simply want to get away from the ranch. I want you to feel free to come to my home anytime. I've extravagantly installed a tennis court in my backyard—it's a passion of mine. If I should happen to be gone, you're more than welcome to use it anyway."

A reddening pink crept into Kerry's cheeks as she lowered her gaze to the china cup in her lap. "It's very kind of you to offer, but I'm afraid I don't know how to play tennis. You see, I'm really not athletically inclined."

Jill's lips parted slightly in dawning discovery. How could she have been so blind? Riordan hadn't really been interested in separating Jill from the group to make her feel unwelcome. He had wanted her away from Kerry while he subtly pointed to Todd how little he and Kerry had in common.

"Good lord, Kerry!" Sheena exclaimed with cutting laughter. "You don't know how to swim or play tennis. You don't like riding. What are you going to do here for a month? You'll go stark raving mad if you spend every day sitting around the house by yourself!"

"You've forgotten Kerry isn't alone." The cup

clattered noisily in its saucer as Jill set it on the small table near her chair. Her blue eyes clashed openly with Riordan's metal gray, letting him know she had seen through his ruse and did not intend to sit silently any longer. "I'm sure we'll find plenty to do to occupy the daytime hours."

"And I'm more than willing to entertain Kerry in the evenings," Todd inserted, his previously uncertain expression changing into a smile. "Tomorrow morning I'll show you around the ranch so you won't get disoriented if you go for a walk. I'll persuade Mary to fix a picnic basket for the afternoon. The beaver pool would be a perfect place to have it."

"I'd like that," Kerry murmured, hesitantly returning his warm smile.

Riordan leaned forward and took a cigarette from the pack on the table. "I'm afraid it won't be possible," he said calmly. His bland expression was directed at the match flame he carried to the cigarette. "I'm shorthanded right now, so I won't be able to let you have a couple of days to unwind from the end of term, Todd. You'll have to be up and out bright and early in the morning."

"What?" A startled frown crossed the youthfully handsome face. "Why are you shorthanded? Who isn't here?"

"Tom Manson. I fired him last week for drinking."

"Tom's been nipping at the bottle for years and we both know it." Todd's hazel eyes darkened with suspicion. "After turning a blind eye to it all this time, why did you suddenly fire him for it?"

"He was drunk last week and nearly set the barn on fire. I wasn't about to give him a second chance to succeed." The level gray eyes dared Todd to challenge his decision. Except for a slight tightening of his mouth in resignation, Todd made no reply as he turned toward Kerry.

"I'm sorry, honey. I guess that takes care of that."

"It's all right," Kerry assured him, her hand finally stopping its nervous twisting of her hair. "We'll do it another day."

"Speaking of other days—" Sheena glaced at the slender gold watch on her wrist "—it isn't too long until tomorrow and I still, unfortunately, have to drive home. I'll get my clothes and other things from the bedroom."

Whose bedroom? Jill wondered cattily as the woman rose·lazily to her feet. Accidentally her gaze met Riordan's. Something of her dislike of Sheena Benton must have been in her expression, because amusement twitched the corners of his hard mouth.

Todd unconsciously broke their vaguely challenging exchange of glances by asking what the agenda would be for the following day. The discussion between the two men stayed on ranch business until Sheena reappeared in the doorway.

"Good night, everybody." Her purring smile swept over all the occupants of the room, stopping on Kerry. "Remember, if you feel lonesome, be sure to call me or come over. It's been a pleasure meeting you. And you, too, Miss Randall." It was added as a deliberate afterthought. Jill's fingers curled. Sheena's catlike actions seemed to be contagious!

"It was kind of you to be here to welcome us, Mrs. Benton," she answered insincerely.

Sheena's gaze narrowed for a fleeting second. "It was my pleasure. Riordan—" a winging brow arched toward him "—will you walk me to my car?"

He didn't reply but rose to his feet. The suffocating tension that had enveloped Jill seemed to leave the room with him. She hadn't realized how stiffly she had been holding herself until she drew a free breath.

A certain aura of confinement remained, probably brought on by inactivity. Jill knew Todd and Kerry wouldn't object if she left them alone. In fact, they'd welcome it.

"I think I'll take the coffee service into the kitchen," she announced without receiving any objections in response.

The kitchen was large and spacious with an old breakfast table and Windsor chairs in the center. Despite the modern appliances, the room retained the old-fashioned charm of the rest of the house.

Mary Rivers waved aside Jill's offer to help clean up the few cups and saucers, insisting that it wouldn't require two pairs of hands. Jill stayed for a few minutes anyway. They talked without saying anything.

When she came away from the room, Jill knew her first impression of the matronly housekeeper had been correct. She was a warm, friendly woman and Jill liked her. She hoped the feeling would be mutual.

As she neared the base of the stairs in the entrance hall, the front door opened and Riordan walked in. Nerve ends tensed instinctively. After a fractional pause in her steps, Jill continued forward, her gaze sweeping coolly over his aloof features.

At the base of the stairs, she made a split-second decision and turned to climb them, aware of the long smooth strides carrying Riordan toward her.

"Are you retreating so early?" he mocked softly.

Jill paused on the first step, her hand resting on the polished banister, but she didn't turn around.

"It's been a long day." Silently she added that it promised to be a long month, especially if tonight was any example of what she was to expect.

"Is something wrong, Miss Randall?" Again, ridiculing amusement dominated his voice. Only this time he was at the stairs, stepping to the banister, putting himself in her line of vision.

"Nothing," she shrugged, her gaze striking blue sparks as it clashed with the flint gray hardness of his. Pointedly she directed her attention to the quirking corner of his mouth and the faint smear of lipstick. "You should suggest that Mrs. Benton blot her lipstick. It isn't so likely to rub off."

The grooves around his mouth deepened as Riordan made no move to wipe away the lipstick trace. "The evening hasn't been very enjoyable for you, has it? You're used to a cluster of admirers, I'm sure, but spare tires are sometimes flat. Maybe after a month you'll get used to it."

It was one of those horrible moments when words

deserted Jill. An hour from now she would be able to think of a suitably cutting retort that she could have made. Seething with impotent anger, she couldn't keep her voice from trembling.

"Please tell Kerry that I'm tired and have gone up to my room."

"Of course." Riordan inclined his head with patronizing politeness, the sardonic smile laughing at her excuse.

Her legs were shaking, but they still managed to carry her swiftly up the stairs to her room. Although she wasn't tired, she changed into nightclothes and climbed into bed anyway.

Later she heard Kerry and Todd bidding each other good night in the hall and the closing of their respective bedroom doors. It seemed as if she lay awake a long time after that before drifting to sleep, but she never heard Riordan come up the stairs.

AFTER A WEEK, life at the ranch fell into a pattern. The daylight hours were the ones that brought the most pleasure to Jill. She and Kerry often took exploratory walks in the morning, discovering the beaver pool and other places, but wisely keeping the ranch buildings in sight at all times. In the afternoons they lazed in the sun or helped Mary when she would let them. It wasn't a demanding routine but a welcome change from the hectic college schedule of classes and study.

As Jill had expected, Sheena stopped over. Both of her visits coincided with times that Riordan was at the house—deliberately planned, Jill was sure. Neither visit had changed Jill's opinion of the woman.

Part of Jill's pleasure was derived from the fact that Riordan was gone from the house with the rising of the sun. Todd, too, of course. Generally it was nearly dark before they returned. On only three days had they been close enough to the ranch house to return for lunch, an event that Kerry looked forward to and Jill dreaded.

The evenings were blessedly short. By the time Riordan and Todd returned, showered away the day's dirt and had eaten dinner, it was nearly time to go to bed. Still, it was more time in Riordan's company than Jill wanted to spend. He was constantly baiting her with a word or a look guaranteed to set her teeth on edge. Kerry he virtually ignored, intimidating her into gaucherie merely with his presence.

Since the object of this visit was ostensibly for Riordan to get to know Kerry better, his indifference annoyed Jill, but she was helpless to do anything about it. She could hardly point out Kerry's good qualities as if her friend was a slave on an auction block.

The Tiffany glass pane in the living-room window lacked its usual brilliant color. The thunderheads concealing the mountain peaks had completely blocked out the sun. The fat drops that had been ricocheting off the windows had turned into a sheeting downpour of rain. Serrated bolts of lightning were followed by rolling explosions of thunder that rattled the window panes.

Todd had dashed into the house alone more than a quarter of an hour ago, drenched to the skin. Jill hadn't cared where Riordan was. She was curled in a corner of the living-room sofa staring at the portrait above the fireplace, wondering how that beautiful woman could mother two so very different sons.

"Hi, where's Kerry?" Todd walked into the living room, tucking a clean shirt into his dry trousers.

His brown hair was still damp, gleaming almost as black as Riordan's. For an instant the resemblance between the two brothers was strong. It vanished when Jill met the friendly hazel eyes.

"In the kitchen, making you some hot chocolate," she replied.

"That woman is going to make some man a great wife," he sighed, sinking into the wing chair opposite the sofa. A crack of lightning was ominously close. "Rain, rain, rain!" A smile of contentment turned up his mouth. "I was beginning to think I was never going to have an afternoon off. What have you been doing this lovely rainy day, Jill?"

Her gaze swept to the portrait. "Reading," she answered absently, although the book had been discarded on the cushion beside her for some time. With a curious frown, she glanced to Todd. "May I ask a nosy question?"

"Ask it and I'll decide whether I want to answer it," he grinned, obviously refreshed and in a jesting mood.

"The portrait of your mother is still hanging above the fireplace. I guess I was wondering why." She tipped her head to one side, watching Todd's teasing smile fade as he turned toward the portrait, a soft admiring affection in his gaze. "She and your father were separated for nearly eighteen years, weren't they?"

"It's always hung there ever since I can remember. And separated isn't really the right word to use." Todd leaned back in his chair, his expression thoughtful when he glanced at Jill. "They lived separately, which isn't quite the same thing. For nine months of the year mom and I lived with her father. In the summer, we came here."

"Every year?"

"Every year," he nodded. "I'd wake up one morning in Helena and Mom would say we were going to the ranch. She never called ahead to say we were coming, but I can't remember a time that dad wasn't there to meet her. It's very hard to explain how very much they loved each other, but they did, genuinely. And every summer it was like a honeymoon. They would laugh, talk in whispers, and dad would steal a kiss every once in a while. I couldn't begin to count the number of times I saw them simply gazing into each other's eyes. Then on an August morning, mom would say we were going back to my grandfather's."

"But why?" Confusion clouded Jill's eyes. "I mean if they loved each other so much, why did they live apart?"

He breathed in deeply and gazed at the portrait. "Mother couldn't stand the isolation of the ranch. She needed people around her. She was gregarious, always wanting to meet new faces. I can remember her telling me how she used to pray for something to break down when she lived here. It didn't matter what it was as long as it required a repairman to fix it and she would have someone new to talk to if only for an hour. For eight years, she said that she kept thinking she would adjust. Finally she couldn't tolerate it any more.''

"It's a miracle they stayed in love all those years. Being separated nine months of every year would put a strain on any relationship,'' she declared with an amazed shake of her blond hair.

"Dad did come to Helena every year at Christmas time for a couple of days. Riordan came, too, until he was about sixteen. On our way up here the other day, you asked me about Riordan as a boy,'' Todd frowned absently. "I think in a way he believed that mother deserted him and dad, even though Riordan realized that she had wanted him to live with her. He never said anything to me, but I imagine he thought she had lovers. She never did, Jill. You can't hide something like that for eighteen years, not even from a small boy, and I lived with her all the time. There was only one man for her and that was my father. It was a very special and rare kind of love they had for each other, and one that was very strong.''

"It had to be,'' Jill agreed, staring at the portrait.

"Do you know what dad used to call her? His butterfly.''

Everything inside Jill seemed to freeze. The chilling that stopped her heartbeat halted the breathing of her lungs. A numbing paralysis spread through her limbs. A resentment that had been manifested in

Riordan's childhood was responsible for his bitter dislike and contempt of her, another butterfly.

"There you are, Todd." Kerry's happy voice came from the open doorway. "I fixed you some hot chocolate. I thought you might like some after your drenching."

"Remind me to marry you," Todd winked, grabbing her hand as she set the cup on the walnut table between the two wing chairs.

"I will," Kerry laughed but with a breathless catch.

Thunder clapped, vibrating the walls.

"Todd!" At the sound of Riordan's commanding voice, Jill nearly jumped off the sofa.

The thunder had evidently drowned out the opening and closing of the front door. He was standing in the doorway, his clothes comparatively dry. A telltale dampness around his shirtsleeves and collar indicated he had been wearing a rain slicker.

"Just because it's raining, it doesn't mean there isn't work to do," he said curtly.

Jill kept her face averted from those discerning gray eyes. All of her senses were reacting to his presence with alarming intensity.

"I've just changed into dry clothes," Todd grumbled in protest.

"If you'd taken your slicker, you wouldn't have got soaked," was the unsympathetic response. "Come on, we might as well sharpen the mower blades."

"There goes my afternoon off!" Sighing, Todd rose from the chair, smiling apologetically at Kerry.

"Thanks for the cocoa, honey, but I'm afraid you'll have to drink it."

When the front door closed behind the two men, a long resigned sigh broke from Kerry's lips. "Here, Jill, you drink it. I don't want it."

The cup was set on the table in front of the sofa. "Hey!" Jill scolded, catching the look of utter depression on her friend's face. "It's not the end of the world. Todd will be back."

"In time for dinner." Kerry stuffed her hands in the pockets of her slacks and walked dejectedly to the window.

"You knew he had to work when we came," Jill reminded her.

"I knew." The downcast chin was raised to stare unseeingly through the rain-sheeted glass.

"Don't let the weather get you down. Why don't we start a fire in the fireplace? That ought to chase away the gloom."

"It's not that." Kerry turned tiredly away from the window. "Haven't you noticed?"

"Noticed what?"

"We've been here seven days and in all that time I've seen Todd alone about a total of one hour. He works from dawn to dusk, never has any free time, and at night his brother is always around."

"And me, too," Jill inserted gently.

She suddenly realized that she had been so anxious to insulate herself from Riordan, she hadn't considered that Todd and Kerry would want to be alone.

And it had been one of her prime objectives on their arrival.

"I'm not blaming you," Kerry assured her quickly.

"I know you're not, but maybe there's something I can do to arrange some time for you and Todd."

"If only there was!" Kerry's brows lifted expressively.

Surprisingly, an opportunity presented itself that evening. Jill had been deliberately pleasant to Riordan at the dinner table, not overly so in case he suspected some ulterior motive. Mostly she attempted to avoid exchanging innuendos, asking questions without becoming too personal.

When the four of them left the table to have coffee in the living room, as had become the custom, Riordan glanced out through the night-darkened windows. "The rain has stopped. We'll have to get out and check the stock tomorrow."

"It isn't raining?" Jill repeated, taking hold of the opportunity. "If you three don't mind, I think I'll skip the coffee. After being in the house all day, a walk sounds very welcome." Riordan was behind her, so he didn't see the wink she gave Kerry.

"Of course not," Kerry answered, a secret sparkle of understanding in her brown eyes.

"I'll get my sweater." Jill started for the stairs and paused. "I'd better see if Mary has a flashlight I can borrow." She laughed lightly. "I don't want to stumble over something and break a leg in the dark."

"I'll come with you," Riordan said.

"There's no need," she refused quickly. "I'll be all right by myself, honestly."

"I'm sure you would be, but I'll come with you just the same." The chiseled features were aloofly set, a faintly sardonic quirk to the ruthless mouth.

Jill hesitated, deliberately giving the impression that she would like to argue the point. Riordan wasn't as easy to manipulate as some men she had known.

"All right." She gave in after letting him hold her wavering gaze with his long measuring look. "I'll get my sweater."

A pulse was throbbing much too wildly in her throat when she descended the stairs, sweater in hand. She blamed it on the disturbing gray eyes watching every step. Her breathless smile was genuine. She had taken the time to run a brush through her hair and add the shimmer of gloss to her lips.

With no false modesty, she knew she presented an alluringly innocent picture. This time, unlike the previous time she had tried to trick him, the emphasis was on the alluring rather than the innocent. He might despise butterflies, but Riordan was human—Sheena proved that.

Her feet carried her lightly across the hall and through the door he held open. She paused outside long enough for him to close the door and turn to join her. Then, leading the way, she moved down the few steps to the stone walk. As she turned onto the lane, she pretended to ignore the man walking a fraction of a pace behind her.

The course of the rutted lane across the meadow

had been a deliberate choice. Here she would be walking directly in the moonlight, its silver gleam catching the sheen of her lips and accenting the blondness of her hair.

Her eyes swept the panoramic landscape. It wasn't necessary to pretend an enchantment with the night's beauty. A lopsided moon was directly in front of them, dominating the starfire of the black sky. In the distance, Jill could see the bank of thunderclouds and the lightning that played hide and seek within.

"It's beautiful," she murmured as if to herself, but she had not forgotten for one instant that Riordan was with her.

"Yes."

The dry cynicism startled Jill. A glance at that strong profile told her that he was untouched by the beauty of the night or her. As unyielding as his expression was, the moonlight had softened the rugged lines, giving him a dangerous, ruthless kind of attraction.

Jill had forgotten how tall he was and the way his well-proportioned frame gave a deceptive impression of leanness. Strolling beside him the way she was, she was aware of the solid muscles in his arms, chest and legs.

"Don't you think it's beautiful?" She paused when he did, questioning the reason for his less than enthusiastic response.

A match flamed to the end of a cigarette and was shaken out. His silver gaze swung to her face, metallic and reflecting.

"Are you angling for a compliment?" Riordan taunted.

"A compliment?" she repeated blankly.

"Wasn't I supposed to be affected by the vision of your loveliness in the moonlight?" His mouth twisted into a jeering smile.

Anger sparked in her eyes as she unflinchingly met his steady look. "No." Her voice was calm and completely indifferent.

Smoothly she started forward, feeling his doubting gaze on her profile and knowing that she *had* intended to prompt some measure of admiration. She'd cut off her arm before she would admit that.

"Aren't we supposed to talk about Todd and Kerry?" The sarcastic inflection of his low voice whipped at the raw edges of her temper.

Jill kept walking, gazing at the mountain meadow without seeing anything. "If you want to," she shrugged carelessly.

"Isn't that why you invited me along?"

"I didn't invite you along, Riordan. You invited yourself," she reminded him, sending him a complacent glance through the sweep of her lashes.

His mouth twitched with amusement. "I know you wanted me to come with you. I just haven't figured why." A gauzy cloud of smoke was blown ahead of them, the wispy trail waiting to ensnare Jill.

"My reason for taking this walk is nothing more complicated than a desire to be outdoors in the fresh air," she defended airily. She tossed her head back to send him a glittering look. "The evening is much too peaceful to start an argument with you."

"You've been conciliatory all evening. Why, Jill?" The husky issuance of her name started a disturbing reaction in her stomach.

"I've already told you."

"You've given a reason, but you haven't told the truth."

The man was too perceptive by far. "Why don't you tell me what the truth is?" she challenged lightly.

"I imagine a girl as beautiful as you has become accustomed to large quantities of admiration from the opposite sex. After a week here, you might be in need of a man's company," Riordan suggested mockingly. "A casual flirtation to keep in practice."

"And I'm supposed to have tricked you into coming with me for that purpose?" Jill demanded, her head thrown back, the sheen of her blond hair glistening palely in the moonlight.

"You've picked a romantic setting," he taunted. "A walk in the moonlight on a path that takes us some distance from the house, just the two of us—alone."

She swallowed involuntarily, glancing furtively around, not realizing how far they had walked from the ranch house. They were very much alone, surrounded by meadow and moonlight.

"If that was my intention, I would surely have picked a man who at least was attracted to me. You've made your dislike of me very clear," she responded boldly.

"On the contrary, I am attracted to you. I may think

you're a scheming little witch—" his mouth curved into a humorless smile while he lazily inspected her upturned face "—but it doesn't lessen the desire to make love to you. You're a very beautiful woman."

The bluntness of his declaration sent shivers of ice down her spine. "Save your compliments for Sheena. I'm sure she would appreciate them much more than I do," Jill answered sharply, averting her face.

His thumb and finger caught her chin and turned her back. "Jealous?" Riordan mocked huskily, his eyes glittering over the deepening color in her cheeks that not even the dim light could hide.

Her eyes blazing, she wrenched away from his touch. "You're conceited, arrogant—"

The sheen in his eyes turned to metallic steel as he clamped a hand over her mouth, shutting off the tirade with the swiftness of a slicing blade. Her hands came up to tear his fingers away and she was crushed against his chest.

"I wondered how long it would take before you lost your temper." Slowly he removed his hand. "You can scream all you want. There isn't anyone around to hear you."

"Let me go!" Jill hissed.

Riordan smiled coldly, lacing his fingers through her hair to prevent her from twisting her face away. His mouth descended toward her and Jill was helpless to avoid it. A gasp of protest was torn from her throat as he nuzzled the throbbing pulse in her neck.

"Make your token resistance if you must," he jeered, raising havoc with her heartbeat as he nibbled at her ear, "but you know you intended this to happen all along."

"No," she denied.

His mouth trailed over her cheek to taste the corner of her lips, the warmth of his breath caressing her skin.

"Why else did you want me to come with you?" Riordan smiled with arrogant conceit.

The tantalizing closeness of his mouth, sensually touching without taking, was unnerving. A purely physical reaction started a trembling through her limbs.

"Don't!" She spoke against his mouth, fire leaping somewhere inside her. "I left the h-house because I wanted privacy—"

"Naturally," he agreed.

"No. Privacy for Todd and Kerry," Jill explained desperately. "I . . . I thought they should have some time alone. That's why I wanted you to come with me."

His head raised from hers, a brow arching in satisfaction. "Now I know the truth," he murmured, relaxing his hold so she could pull free.

Staring at him, Jill bit into her lip still burning from the nearness of his. "You tricked me, didn't you?" she accused in a shallow breath. "You never intended to try to seduce me."

"Could I have?" The grooves around his mouth deepened.

"No!" She spun away.

Her flesh still tingled from the imprint of his male

form and there was a funny empty ache in the pit of her stomach. Could he, a tiny voice inside asked.

"No!" The second vigorous denial was made to the voice.

"We'd better head back to the house," Riordan said with silent laughter in his voice, "while you're still trying to make up your mind. If you aren't convinced, then I may become curious enough to find out for myself."

It sounded very much like a threat to Jill. Sometimes it was better to retreat and lose a battle than to stay and lose a war. Right now Riordan was much too disturbing an influence for her to think straight.

As they entered the house with Jill a hurried step ahead of Riordan, Kerry walked out of the living room. There was no inner glow to her expression as Jill had expected. For a moment she forgot her own haste to reach the safety of the bedroom.

"Where's Todd?" Jill glanced curiously toward the living room. A frown appeared on her forehead as she tried to guess if the two had quarreled.

"He's in the living room," Kerry answered tightly, her lips thinning in irritation. "He was so tired he fell asleep twenty minutes ago."

Jill's lashes fluttered shut in sighing disbelief. A low throaty chuckle sounded behind her, rolling into outright laughter. She darted an angry look at Riordan, catching the crinkling of his eyes at the corners, the merry glint of gray in the pupils and the broad, laughing smile. It was a Riordan that she had never seen before.

A wickedness entered the merry glint. "Ah, the irony of it, Jill," he concluded with a wry shake of his ebony dark head.

"What's so funny?" Kerry frowned after Riordan had strode away, still smiling, toward the rear of the house.

Jill put a hand to her mussed hair, a faint smile tugging the corners of her mouth. "Don't ask, Kerry," she answered with a short sighing laugh. "From your viewpoint, I don't think it would be very funny."

CHAPTER SIX

"WE'VE CHANGED THE BEDDING in all the rooms except Riordan's, Mary," Jill announced, tucking an escaping wisp of hair under her old-fashioned blue bandanna. "I'm afraid we couldn't figure out which room was his."

Mary Rivers was on her hands and knees in the hallway cleaning and polishing the woodwork. She straightened stiffly upright, a hand pushing against the small of her back.

"I already took care of his room. He sleeps downstairs in the rear . . . I didn't think to mention it. Old age, I expect."

"Would you want me to put the sheets in the washer?" Kerry asked, holding the armload in front of her.

"You girls have done enough. You're guests in this house, not daily help." The housekeeper shook her head in refusal of the offer.

"We enjoy helping," Jill insisted.

"It's much better than sitting around doing nothing. At least this way we can be useful," Kerry added. "Besides, what's involved in washing sheets? All I have to do is stick them in the washer, add detergent and push a button.''

''While she's doing that, I can help you with this woodwork.'' Without allowing time for a protest, Jill bent over to pick up the cloth and polish at Mary Rivers's feet.

''I can't let you girls do this.'' The housekeeper tried to take the cleaning items from Jill's hand, but she held them out of reach.

''How are you going to stop us?'' Kerry asked pertly, turning down the hall toward the kitchen and the utility room beyond it.

''Come on, Mary,'' Jill coaxed. ''Let us help. You said yourself that by the time you do the cooking and regular cleaning, you're lucky to have the spring housecleaning done by fall. We've been here over ten days. We can't keep doing nothing while you work.''

''You make the beds and straighten your own rooms. That's enough of a help to me.''

''Let us help you with other things. Not all the time but every once in a while, like now. We've little else to do with our time,'' Jill pointed out.

''I give up!'' Mary lifted her hands in the air in surrender. ''I'll get another polishing cloth and we'll both clean this entrance hall.''

''It's a deal,'' Jill smiled. ''I'll do the woodwork near the floor so you won't have be getting up and down so much. You can do that carving around the wainscoting.''

After two hours of scooting along the floor on her hands and knees, Jill's muscles in her back, shoulders and arms started to protest. She hurt, but it was a good kind of hurt, if that was possible. The work was certainly an outlet for the restlessness that had been plaguing both girls.

The evenings had returned to their former pattern with Riordan dominating, by his presence, the other three. Jill didn't make any more attempts to maneuver Riordan away from Todd and Kerry.

Naturally Kerry had, bit by bit, wheedled an account of Jill's disastrous single attempt. Jill never admitted that she had actually thought Riordan intended to seduce her or that, for a few traitorous moments, her flesh had been tempted to respond to his teasing caresses.

Without these pertinent facts, Kerry had seen the ironic humor of the event. While Jill had been ineffectually trying to fend off Riordan's advances—as Kerry believed they were—she had been listening to Todd snore.

The end result of the episode for Jill had been an increasing awareness of her masculine host. She was certain that Riordan could, if he wanted to, arouse her physically as no other man had done. She had always been the one in control of all aspects of a relationship, and she didn't like the sensation of being so vulnerable. He didn't like butterflies. It was a possibility that he might some day decide to tarnish her wings.

A shiver danced over her skin as she remembered the tantalizing warmth of his mouth just barely brushing hers. A dangerous curiosity kept wondering what it would be like to be kissed by him—not the degrading, punishing kiss he had subjected her to when they first met, but a kiss of passion.

And there was the silent challenge, too. Every man she had ever gone after, she had got. But what about Riordan? Was he the exception to the rule?

There was a jingling in the hallway behind her. Brushing a stray strand of hair away from her eyes, Jill started to turn around. What a silly time for Kerry to put on a bracelet, she thought. Then the jingling was accompanied by the sound of long, angry strides closing on her. There was a fleeting glimpse of Riordan's uncompromising and forbidding features.

In the next second, Jill's wrist was seized in a vice grip and she was yanked to her feet, unaware of the startled gasping cry that came from her throat. Her legs were momentarily too numb from the crawling position to support her. She sought to steady herself against his chest with her free hand.

"What the hell is going on here!" Riordan shouted. He pulled the hand from his chest to tear away the polishing cloth unconsciously still clutched in her fingers and hurl it to the far side of the hall. "Mary!"

Jill stumbled heavily against him, her heart lurching as she came against the solid wall of muscle. His arm automatically released her wrist and circled her waist to catch her, taking her full weight as if it were no more than a child's.

The suddenness of the forced movement had thrown her head back, her stunned gaze staring into his narrowed eyes darkened like turbulent thunderclouds. She shuddered at the violence contained within.

"Mary, what's the meaning of this?" Thunder growled threateningly in his voice. "And you'd better have a damned good explanation!"

His strong male scent was all around Jill, filling her senses to the exclusion of everything but his nearness. It seemed to take all her strength to look away from the compelling features so close to her own and focus on the housekeeper who was the recipient of his stormy gaze. Mary Rivers didn't appear intimidated by his anger. Instinctively Jill leaped to her defense anyway.

"I was helping," she inserted breathlessly.

Riordan's gaze slashed to her for a paralyzing second. "Shut up, Jill. Mary is perfectly capable of answering for herself." His attention was again riveted on the housekeeper. "Well?"

"The girls offered to help," she answered simply.

"You've been working, too?" An accusing glance was thrown over his shoulder. Jill could barely see Kerry hovering uncertainly near the stairs, her brown eyes rounded and stunned at the sight of Jill a captive of this snarling lion.

"I . . . was doing the wash," she murmured.

Riordan muttered an imprecation under his breath. "I am only going to say this once, Mary." A muscle worked convulsively in his strong jaw. "They are my guests in my house and I will not have guests crawling around on their hands and knees cleaning woodwork or washing clothes!"

Mary Rivers stood calmly before him, straight and tall, her hands clasped in front of her. "They're strong, healthy girls, Riordan. You can't expect them to sit in this house day after day twidding their thumbs."

"I don't give a damn what they do. I will not have them working like hired help in this house. Is that clear?"

"How can you stop us?" Jill breathed in challenge. "Mary tried and she couldn't. You weren't even here. I took the cloth and polish away from her and demanded to help."

The arm around her waist tightened, crushing her more firmly against his rippling muscles. The hard glint in his eyes that commanded her silence gave Jill the impression that he would like to snap her in two.

"Stay out of this." Narrowed slits of steel sliced across Jill's flushed face, then cut swiftly back to Mary. "Have I made myself clear?"

"I'm not to blame for this." The housekeeper held his gaze without flinching. "As you pointed out, they're guests in this house. It's your responsibility and not mine to see that they're entertained. If you choose to neglect that, you have no right to lose your temper because they found their own way to amuse themselves and fill the empty time."

"And you would do well, Mary—" Jill was cast away from him, sagging limply against the wall like a rag doll as Riordan turned to tower above the housekeeper "—to remember that you are not a part of the family, but a paid employee!"

The spurs on his boots jingled noisily again as long strides carried him to the door. Jill flinched at the explosive slamming of the door, half expecting the rattling windows to shatter from the impact. Her gaze shifted automatically to the housekeeper silently staring at the door.

"I'm sorry, Mary," she offered sincerely, strength finally beginning to flow through her limbs. "We never intended to get you into trouble."

"He'll get over it." Mary Rivers shrugged philosophically. A twinkle sparkled in her dark eyes. "But in the meantime I think you'd better leave the housework to me until he cools down at least!"

The atmosphere in the house remained electrified. There wasn't any room that possessed an immunity to the invisible tension. Dinner that evening was an awkward affair.

Riordan's disposition hadn't improved. A black mood seemed to hover about the house during dinner. Not even his unexpected departure from the house after the meal put any of them at ease. The tension remained in the house into the following day. Wanting to defy him, Jill was still hesitant to offer again to help Mary. She wasn't quite as convinced as Mary that Riordan was going to get over his anger.

Perhaps that was why his announcement the following night at the dinner table came as such a surprise. Her lips were slightly parted in disbelief as she continued to stare at him.

"A trail ride?" Todd echoed the words Riordan had just spoken.

Riordan appeared indifferent to the stunned reaction his suggestion had met. "I thought we could leave first thing Monday morning. That will give the girls some time to get accustomed to the horses. We can only be gone two days."

"Horses?" Kerry swallowed.

A black brow arched briefly in cynical amusement. "Yes, horses," Riordan affirmed. "Unless you want to walk to the top of the mountain?"

"No, of course not," Kerry rushed nervously, glancing to Jill to see her reaction.

"You did say you could ride," he reminded Kerry pointedly.

"She can ride well enough," Todd answered for her, reaching out to cover Kerry's hand. "I'll pick out a nice, gentle mount for you."

"And you, Jill?" Riordan drawled, his impassive gray eyes shifting to her. "Can you ride, or will you require a nice, gentle mount, too?"

Despite the casualness of his voice, there was a decided bite underlining the question. She tried to fathom his expression without success. She still couldn't believe that he sincerely meant to go through with it.

"I can ride." Her reply was marred by uncertainty.

"You don't sound very enthusiastic," he commented dryly.

"Maybe—" Jill breathed in deeply, drawing on her reserve of bold courage "—because I don't think the invitation for this trail ride was offered willingly."

"Jill!" whispered Kerry in a shocked plea for caution.

"You believe that Mary's little speech yesterday reminding me of my responsibilities as host black-mailed me into suggesting this?" Riordan challenged, leaning back in his chair and regarding Jill thought-fully from his mask of aloofness.

"Yes, I do," she nodded.

"Well, you're quite right in believing that." The hard line of his mouth quirked briefly as he arro-gantly inclined his head in acknowledgement. "The question remains, do you want to go?"

Jill definitely wanted to go. Her brother had been the last one to take her on a trip into the high country around her home in Yellowstone. But this wasn't exactly Kerry's cup of tea. Of course, her friend would go to the moon if Todd asked.

Her chin raised thoughtfully, as she met Riordan's narrowed gaze of watchfulness. He was very well aware of Kerry's timidity toward animals, especially something as large as a horse, and her lack of an adventurous streak that made Kerry prefer the secu-rity of a house to the unknowns of the wilderness. Jill had been the one who had prompted the exploring walks around the ranch.

Kerry's only dissatisfaction in their stay here had been she hadn't seen as much of Todd as she wanted. She would have been content to potter around the house.

Jill didn't condemn Kerry for being unwilling to experience other worlds, but Riordan did. He considered it a fatal flaw for his brother's prospective bride to have. It was time he learned that Kerry had a lot of spunk, Jill decided. However much Kerry wanted the security of a house, she would, without a grumble, go wherever Todd led her. Kerry was like a lot of pioneer women had been—she could make a home wherever her man was.

If Riordan expected to hear Kerry complain about the hardships of the long ride and camping out, or give way to fits of terror at crawling insects and the night cries of wild animals, he was going to be in for a surprise. A secret smile teased the corners of her mouth.

"Yes," Jill finally responded to his question with a decisive nod of her head, "I would like to go."

"It's settled, then," Riordan stated, a faint glitter of curiosity at the almost complacent look on Jill's face. "I'll start making the necessary arrangements."

Dawn was only splintering the sky when they pointed their horses away from the ranch buildings toward the shadowed mountain slopes three days later. Fresh and eager for the trail, Jill's horse snorted, sending vapor clouds into the brisk morning air. She glanced behind her at the wide path they had left in the dew-heavy grass of the meadow.

The silence seemed almost enchanted. Only it wasn't really silent. The grass swished beneath the horses' hooves, scattering diamond droplets of dew. All around was the chirping wake-up call of the birds. Loudest of all was the rhythmic creak of saddle leather.

"Having second thoughts?" Riordan asked in a low voice.

The roofs of the ranch buildings had almost disappeared behind the rise in the meadow as Jill faced the front again. There was a serene glow in her expression when she glanced at Riordan riding beside her, leading the packhorse carrying their supplies.

"None at all," she assured the mocking gray eyes playing over her face.

The faint glow of pale yellow lasted only a few short minutes more before the sun popped above the craggy peaks to the east. The mountain seemed to catch the light of the rising sun, reflecting the golden hues. By the time they reached the foothills, it was well up in the sky, flooding the forested slopes with brilliant sunshine, piercing the foliage with golden streamers of light.

The delicate scent of pines dominated the air as the four riders entered the forest. Riordan led the way through the moderately dense growth with Jill behind him, followed by Kerry and Todd bringing up the rear. The narrow, weaving route through the trees was traversed single file which made conversation almost impossible. Jill didn't mind. She savored the solitude of her own thoughts.

The private glimpses of wildlife were many. A jay followed them for some distance through the trees as if inspecting the invaders of his domain. Squirrels hid behind trunks waiting for them to pass before resuming their endless search for food.

At the edge of a small forest glade, Jill's horse

stopped. She had been watching a squirrel peering warily around a trunk. Glancing forward, she saw that Riordan had reined in his horse and checked the packhorse's progress. Curious, she looked beyond him.

In the sun-drenched glade, two deer stared motionless in their direction. Then, with a flick of a white tail, they bounded away, gracefully leaping through the tall rippling grass dotted with brilliant reds and yellows of wildflowers.

Without a word or glance being exchanged with the others, Riordan nudged his bay horse into the open. Jill followed keeping single file and not attempting to draw level with him. For a moment, she ignored the scenery and concentrated on the wide shoulders ahead of her.

Riordan sat with casual ease, a part of the horse and environment, the untamed look about him more pronounced than before. The warmth of the sun had made itself felt and his suede jacket was swinging open. A wild tremor shook her senses as she caught a glimpse of his rugged profile. With the golden sun striking sparks off the chiseled features of his strong jaw and the faintly ruthless line of his mouth, his virile attraction pulled her like a powerful magnet.

Riordan was in his element in this wilderness country, Jill told herself, trying to shake away her purely physical reaction. Her blue eyes swung determinedly away from him to focus again on the landscape they rode through. But more and more often as the morning wore on, her gaze was drawn to the man riding in the lead.

Farther on, the trees began to thin out, giving way to a grassy plateau studded with rocks and colored with mountain wildflowers. It seemed as if their steady climb should have gained them great height, but craggy mountain peaks towered all around them. This was only an insignificant hill dwarfed by its bigger brothers, connected by a dipping ridge to their slopes.

Yet the crest of the hill beckoned Jill. Behind her, the valley floor was a twisting corridor through the fortress walls of the mountains. The vista at the top of the hill promised a look at it and the untouched wilderness beyond. She urged her horse even with Riordan, meeting his sideways glance of inquiry, a black brow lifting slightly.

"Are we riding to the top of the hill?" she asked.

The breathlessness in her question was merely from the exhilaration of the ride. It had nothing to do with the quicksilver glitter in his considering look, she told herself.

"We can." He reined in his horse and turned sideways in the saddle toward the slower couple following them. "We're going to the top, Todd."

Todd waved them on. "We'll meet you at the ridgeback."

That wasn't what Jill had in mind. She had intended that the four of them share the view, but she could hardly protest now. Riordan took a wrap on the packhorse's lead rope. Clicking to it, he touched a spur to his bay's flank, and the horse's striding walk obediently extended into a reaching trot. Jill followed.

The crest of the hill was farther and steeper than she had guessed. A lone pine growing out of an outcropping of jagged rock at the top seemed to be the point to which Riordan was taking her. The last few yards she gave her horse his head to pick his way over the stony ground, always climbing.

"I didn't realize it was so far," she said when her horse stopped beside Riordan's at the top. Her gaze was already sweeping the breathtaking panorama. "But it was worth it."

The ranch buildings far below were almost totally hidden by the windbreak of pines. The verdant meadow stretched like a curling green ribbon on the valley floor. The unexplored horizon on the opposite side of the hill was dominated by snow-capped peaks and virgin valleys, wild and unscarred by man, stunning in their casual grandeur.

Riordan dismounted, looping the rope to the packhorse around his saddle horn. "We'll take a breather here and give the horses a rest."

Her dismount was considerably less graceful than his, stiff muscles unaccustomed to extended periods of riding making their protest felt. All of that was forgotten as she spied a dark shape in the crystal blue sky.

"Riordan, look!" she whispered excitedly. He was loosening the cinch on his saddle and paused to follow her pointing finger. "Is it an eagle or a hawk?"

"An eagle." His sharp gaze remained fixed on the wide span of wings. Unconsciously Jill moved closer, her blood racing with excitement. "I'd say it's a bald eagle. This is one of the few regions you can still find them where they haven't been driven out by civilization."

She was unable to take her eyes from the eagle soaring high on the wind currents above the mountains. "I don't know how anyone can claim to be rich if they haven't seen an eagle flying wild and free."

"That's a profound statement."

Something in his voice drew her gaze. Behind the lazily piercing quality of his eyes, she suspected she saw a glint of admiration. The sight of the eagle had made her spirits buoyantly light. It was like a heady wine, making her feel decidedly reckless.

"You mean coming from me," she returned boldly, "you don't expect such statements."

Riordan moved lazily around to her horse. A stirrup was laid over the saddle while he loosened the cinch. A breeze lifted the tousled wings of her hair, spinning wisps of burnished gold in the sunlight.

"Maneuvering again, Jill?" he taunted softly.

Unbuttoning her medium-weight jacket of lined blue corduroy, she pushed it back so the refreshing breeze could reach her skin.

"I don't know what you mean," she shrugged carelessly.

"You knew when you suggested we come to the top of this hill that Kerry wouldn't willingly make any side trails on her horse." Patting the horse's neck, he ducked beneath its head to stand beside Jill. "Weren't you arranging for her to be alone with Todd?"

"If you say so." With a contented sigh, she tilted her face to the sun, letting its warm rays spill over her, with her hands on her hips holding the jacket open. "I'm in much too good a mood to argue with you, Riordan."

"I wasn't arguing," he replied smoothly.

"Weren't you?" Amusement dimpled her cheeks.

Glancing through the gold tips of her lashes, she met his aloofly mocking eyes. They trailed slowly over her face down her neck to her blouse, dwelling on the material straining over the jutting roundness of her breasts. A silvery flame seemed to lick through the material, igniting a rush of warmth in her veins.

"I believe you're trying to flirt with me," he drawled, stepping by her to remove a canteen from his saddle.

Studying the jet black hair that curled around his collar, she tipped her head to one side, feeling playfully bold. "And if I am?"

He unscrewed the lid of the canteen and handed it to her, his mouth quirking. "I think you're outclassed."

Her azure eyes sparkled brightly over the rim of the canteen as she took a swallow of the cool water. Her senses were vibrantly alert and ready to take up the challenge. Jill gave him back the canteen.

"I don't think you know me very well," she retorted softly, almost in warning.

Had he not raised the canteen to his mouth at that moment, Riordan would have seen the mischief glittering in her eyes. At precisely the right second, she lifted her hand and tipped the canteen, spilling water over his face. Despite the dangerous glitter in the gray eyes, she couldn't keep from laughing.

"Why, you little minx!" Riordan growled, but without real anger. The lid was replaced on the canteen as he took a threatening step toward her.

The hasty, laughing step Jill took backwards sent her bumping into his horse, who moved only a protesting inch. She tried to elude his reaching hands and failed as they dug into the soft flesh of her upper arms.

"I'm sorry, Riordan, honestly." But the bubbling amusement that remained in her voice belied the assertion. "I couldn't help it."

Her forearms were pressed against his chest as she laughingly tried to struggle free of his hold. Swinging her head back, she turned her mirthful eyes to his face.

The smoldering light in his eyes was not from anger and the smile slowly faded from her lips. Her gaze slid to his mouth, so hard, so masculine, and so close, and resistance ebbed with a rush.

In the next instant, her hands were curling around his neck and his mouth was closing over hers with a savage insistence. Her lips parted voluntarily in response to his passionate demand. Hands slipped beneath her jacket, sliding smoothly to her back, arching and molding her closer to his male outline.

Any sense of inhibition was forgotten as she yielded to his expert caresses. Primitive desire seared through her veins. Shivers of excitement danced over her skin as he minutely explored the hollow of her throat and the pulsing cord in her neck. Her breast seemed to swell as his hands cupped its roundness, arousing previously unknown longing for a more intimate caress. His mouth was hungry and possessive when it returned to hers.

The clatter of hooves against stone shattered the erotic spell. "Riordan, are you coming or not?" Todd called, still some distance away, the pine tree and the horse shielding them from his view.

As he lifted his head reluctantly, Riordan's hands slid to her waist, holding her against him. Jill nestled her head against his chest, a soft smile curving the lips that still throbbed from his ardent kiss.

"We'll be right there," Riordan called in a voice that was husky and disturbed.

Excitement shivered over her skin. Beneath her head she could feel his ragged breathing and hear the uneven beat of his heart, very much in tempo with her own. She could have him.

In that exultant moment, she knew she could bring this man to his knees. It mattered little that he disliked her because now she knew he desired her. The knowledge provided an immense power she could use to gain her own ends.

Then Riordan was setting her away from him and walking to the horses to tighten the cinches. Outwardly he seemed completely unmoved by the charged embrace they had just shared. The gray eyes were cool and aloof, like impenetrable granite, when they met the brightness of hers. His control was remarkable. If she hadn't had those few seconds in his arms after he had broken off the kiss, she might not have guessed that she had so successfully aroused him.

"Mount up," he said, swinging into his own saddle.

His eyes narrowed thoughtfully as Jill gave him a bemused smile and complied with his order. This trail ride was going to be much more interesting and exciting than she had thought. She met his gaze with an alluring sweep of her long lashes, then moved her horse into the lead.

CHAPTER SEVEN

THE GREEN MEADOW was nestled high in the mountains, a miniature valley where the mountain hesitated before soaring toward the sun. Cutting a path near the encroaching forest, a stream tumbled joyously over itself, crystal clear and cold from melting snow.

"I almost wish we never had to leave." Jill turned regretfully away from the scene.

"Do you feel like going primitive?" The gray eyes slid to her briefly as Riordan pulled the saddle from Kerry's mount.

"Something like that," she agreed, smiling at his amused mockery. "What's wrong with returning to nature and the basics?"

"It's easy to do as long as you've brought supplies, but not quite so romantic when you have to forage for food like any other animal." He set the saddle out of the way and tossed a short blanket to Jill. "Rub the horse down and make sure he's dry."

The horse stood docilely as she began to wipe dry the dark stain of perspiration where the saddle and pad had lain. "So you don't think I would like the life in the rugged outdoors?"

As he glanced over the seat of Todd's saddle, his mouth twisted dryly. "You tell me. After a month, your nails would be broken, your hands would be rough and callused. That beautiful complexion of yours would probably be burned by the sun. And who would fix your shiny golden hair?"

Jill laughed. "Why couldn't you have pointed out the hardships and dangers? You could have attacked something other than my vanity." Inside she was secretly pleased that he had noticed so much about her.

"Want some help, Riordan?" Todd paused in front of the horse his brother was now rubbing down. "The camp is all set up and Kerry is gathering more firewood from the deadfall."

"No," Riordan answered after glancing at the site that had been chosen for the night's camp. "You might was well get those telescoping rods from the pack and start catching our supper. Jill and I will finish up here."

"What will we eat if Todd doesn't catch any trout?" she challenged lightly when they were again alone with the horses.

"The contingency menu consists of the old western standby—beans." His eyes crinkled at the corners.

It was only the second time Jill had seen him smile naturally. Her heart quickened at how devastingly attractive it made him.

Tapping the rump of Todd's horse to move it out of the way, Riordan walked around it to his own saddled mount. Jill finished her horse and walked to the bay's head, absently stroking its nose. It blew softly in her hand, the dark brown eyes almost curious in its inspection of her.

"What is your horse's name?" she asked, running her fingers through the horse's tangled black forelock.

Riordan shrugged indifferently. "Boy. Fella." Mockery gleamed silvery bright in the eyes that glanced at her face. "At times, some other names a gentleman shouldn't repeat in front of a woman."

"Doesn't he have a name?" Her head tilted to one side in surprise.

"No. He's only an animal. There are a few horses on the ranch that supposedly have names, the ones that happen to be registered stock." He lifted the saddle off the horse's back, swinging it onto his shoulder and carrying it over to the others. He returned to start rubbing the horse down. "This one is just a mountain-bred horse with no pedigree."

"You honestly don't name your horses?" Jill persisted. "Why?"

The brim of his hat was pulled low, throwing his face into shadow. She couldn't be certain, but she thought she saw his expression momentarily harden. For long seconds he didn't answer. She thought he was going to ignore her question altogether.

"I was about five when Dad gave me my first horse, a buckskin named Yellowstone Joe. I suppose like any boy I imagined he was the best horse in the world. When I was twelve, one Indian summer day I rode him into the mountains to go hunting. I didn't pay any attention to the time until I realized that it was afternoon. I was miles from the ranch with little chance of making it back before dark, unless I took a short cut. It meant going down a steep slide area, with a lot of loose rock. I'd taken Joe down it before, but I'd forgotten to consider that there'd been a storm recently. When we started down, the ground slid out from beneath us. I was thrown clear and rolled to the bottom. Joe was there, too, with both front legs broken.''

Her chest constricted sharply, her blue eyes darkening to mirror the unendurable pain she knew he must have felt. But for all the emotion in his voice, he could have been discussing the weather.

"I was miles from home and help, not that there was anything that could be done for Joe. I couldn't leave him like that, suffering and helpless. I knew he had to be put out of his misery and there wasn't anyone around but me. My marksmanship was off, and it took two shots to kill him. I started walking for home. Dad and a search party found me around nine o'clock that night.''

Jill could hardly distinguish his impassive features through the thick wall of tears, but she could tell his face was turned to her. She could just barely make out the cynical curl of his mouth.

"I don't put names on something I might have to destroy, not any more. Horses are only animals, like cattle you slaughter to eat. It was a lesson that had to be learned,'' Riordan concluded unemotionally.

"Yes. Yes, I see.'' Her voice was choked by the knot in her throat, hoarse and raw with commiseration for that twelve-year-old boy. She knew any minute the tears would spill from her eyes for Riordan to scorn. "I . . . I think I'll go and help . . . Kerry."

"Go ahead," he agreed blandly. "I don't need you. I can finish up here."

Jill wondered if he had stopped needing anybody that day when he was twelve. Two years before that, his mother left him for a reason he couldn't understand. Was it any wonder he had grown up so hard and cynical? She wanted desperately to reach out and gather that little boy in her arms and ease his hurt and grief. Only Riordan wasn't a little boy anymore and he didn't allow himself to be hurt.

Try as she would, Jill couldn't forget the scene his indifferent voice had described. It haunted her, dulling the beauty of the meadow and marring the serenity of the mountain stream. That long-ago event didn't hurt him anymore. She was a fool to let it hurt her.

It didn't change the fact that she had the power to bring him to his knees. She could still use the physical attraction he felt for her to manipulate him into approving of Todd and Kerry's marriage.

A cold, ruthless streak had become embedded in him and he would not hesitate to use any means within his grasp. It wasn't as if she could hurt him again. He was beyond being hurt. He pitied no one, so why should she pity him?

Todd's catch of trout had been spitted and cooked slowly over the glowing embers of the camp fire, then served with canned tomatoes and piping hot bannock biscuits Riordan had fried. It had been a delicious meal, only Jill's appetite had been dulled.

She stared at the speckled gray coffee pot suspended at the side of the fire. Kerry had enlisted Todd's aid in carrying the dishes to the stream to be washed. They had not camped close to the stream because Riordan had explained that animals came down at night to water and he didn't want their camp obstructing the animals' right of way to the stream. The explanation had not put Kerry at ease.

"More coffee?" Riordan stooped beside the fire and refilled his cup from the gray pot.

"No." Jill shook her head absently, her hair catching and reflecting the amber flames of the fire.

From the stream, she heard a startled shriek from Kerry, and Todd's laughing admonition that it was only a harmless raccoon. The corners of Riordan's mouth turned up crookedly.

"Your friend is a little jumpy."

His faintly derogatory tone made blue diamond chips of her eyes, cold and cutting, her heart hardening against him. The time of indecision was thrust away. How dared he criticize Kerry's feelings of fear toward the unknown when he possessed no feelings himself?

"What can you expect, Riordan? Camping in the wilds is completely outside Kerry's experience." Her voice was low and tautly controlled. "It's not so difficult to understand that when you're in alien surroundings with alien creatures known to be wild, you feel apprehensive and not a little bit frightened."

"You aren't frightened."

"No." She turned her head, sharply challenging his hooded look. "But my family camped a lot, backpacking into Yellowstone on weekends, so this isn't a totally new experience for me."

"I see you're still intent on defending your friend." Riordan was in the shadowy circle beyond the fire, the sardonic amusement in his voice mocking her.

"I see you're still intent on breaking them up," Jill retorted smoothly, keeping the anger from her voice.

"I didn't realize butterflies could be so irritable. What's the matter, Jill?" he taunted.

Closing her eyes against the impulse to snap, she took a deep breath, releasing it in a shrugging sigh. "Most butterflies probably never spend a day in the saddle riding up a mountain."

"Stiff?"

"Brilliant deduction," she responded dryly, unconsciously arching the protesting muscles in her back. She stared into the crackling flames of the camp fire.

Pine needles rustled beside her, warning her a second too late of Riordan's approach. As she started to turn, a pair of hands closed firmly over her shoulders and began to spread the taut muscles in her back. A soft moan escaped her startled lips, a mixture of pain and enjoyment.

"If you weren't so prejudiced because Kerry is your friend, you would see that in the long run they aren't suited to each other and you would join forces with me in separating them before they make a big mistake."

His fingers were working magic on her aching flesh.

Jill almost wished there wasn't any need for conversation, but she shook her head determinedly.

"You don't know your brother well, Riordan," she murmured. "I think you somehow believe that he survived the separation of your parents relatively untouched. But you're quite wrong. He's chosen a wife whom he knows will be at his side through anything. If you thought this trail ride was going to point out their differences to Todd, you've failed. If it revealed anything to him, then it's the fact that Kerry joined in without one word of complaint, adjusting as best she could to the surroundings."

"But will she continue to do that?" Riordan mocked softly with underlying sarcasm.

His strong fingers had sent a lethargy creeping through her bones, but at his question Jill stiffened, holding herself motionless as a light flashed in her eyes.

"It isn't Kerry you object to, is it, Riordan?" She answered the quiet demand herself. "It's marriage. No matter who Todd chose, you wouldn't approve."

"No," was his simple and uncaring reply, laced with a touch of amusement.

A short breathy laugh slipped from her throat, not expecting that he should admit it so nonchalantly. Tilting her head to one side, she glanced over her shoulder at his lazily alert expression.

"Do you really despise women that much?" Her eyes searched the carved, imposing features, the enigmatic gray of his eyes.

The hard masculine mouth curved into a cold

taunting smile. "What do you think of men, Jill? Do you admire them? Look up to them? View them as equals? Or do you enjoy twisting them around your pretty little finger and letting them fall when they no longer amuse you?"

His mocking accusation struck too close to the mark. She did tend to play with men, but not cruelly and callously as Riordan suggested. Deep down there was always the hope that the man she went after would be the one she loved. Only with Riordan did she want to be the unfeeling enchantress.

Her tongue nervously moistened her lower lip, unconsciously sensual until she saw the smoldering light darken his eyes. A wicked sparkle flashed in her eyes, enticing and challenging.

"And you, Riordan," she murmured with husky suggestiveness, "do you really despise everything about a woman? Or do you find that they have occasional uses?"

He smiled, recognizing the invitation on her gleaming lips. A dark brow arched, the massaging hands on her back sliding near her ribcage.

"Occasionally," he responded coolly.

Jill fixed her blue gaze on his mouth, feeling her heartbeat quicken. "Like this morning on the hilltop?" Forgotten for the moment was her own naked response to his embrace. Only the memory of the way she had aroused him was considered.

His eyes narrowed thoughtfully as if measuring the strength of the trap she laid for him. The rakish thickness of his hair gleamed blacker in the firelight, a

faint arrogance hardening his impassive features.
"Did you enjoy it?"

"Did you?" Jill breathed.

The hands tightened on her ribs, lifting and turning
her into his arms. The initial shock of having physical
contact again with his hard-muscled chest made her
mind spin. Her head rested against his arm, the tawny
gold of her hair spinning over his shoulder while he
inspected the perfection of her face with slow deliberation. Jill let herself relax pliantly. A hand slid across
her stomach to curve over her hip.

Then the male mouth was closing over hers. That
seductive searing fire that she had somehow forgotten
consumed her again. There was no fierceness in his
touch this time, only a series of long, drugging kisses
calculated to undermine her sensibility to everything
but his virility. A warning bell chimed that she was
losing control. Riordan was seducing her, not the
other way around. The insanity of it was that she
didn't care. She wanted to go on drowning in the
sensual oblivion of his caress.

From this admission came the strength to resist.
With a tremulous gasp, she twisted away from his
mouth using her arms to wedge a space between them.
Her skin felt hot to the touch, the raging fire within
refusing to be banked.

Strong fingers cupped her jaw, tilting her chin
upward. Not daring to meet his eyes for fear she
would be captured by their silvery sheen, Jill stared at
his mouth, so cool, so self-composed compared to the
trembling softness of hers. The tanned fingers trailed

down her neck until his hand rested lightly and deliberately on her breast.

"I want you," Riordan said with soft arrogance.

Yes, he wanted her, Jill acknowledged, but not enough, not yet. Straightening toward him, she let her lips flutter submissively against his mouth as if in surrender to his dominant strength. Then, with a single fluid movement, she was out of his arms and on her feet standing in front of the fire. She could feel him watching the uneven rise and fall of her breasts and tried to stabilize her breathing. Her limbs were treacherously weak beneath her.

Riordan made no move to follow her, his long male length stretched in a half-sitting position, seemingly relaxed and undisturbed. She forced herself to play by the rules of her game, the rules that would allow her to win.

"You'll have to forgive me, Riordan," she sighed, tossing a faint smile over her shoulder. "I'm afraid I got a bit carried away."

"Why should I forgive you for that?" he returned evenly. "I enjoyed it."

"So did I—a little too much." That was the absolute truth, but it served her purpose to say it. "Todd and Kerry should be back soon. Would you care for another cup of coffee?"

"Since there's nothing stronger," he agreed.

Forgetting that the pot had been sitting above the flames for a long time, she tried to pour the coffee without the aid of a pot holder. She had barely closed her fingers around the handle before she released it.

"That's the way to get burned," Riordan drawled, tossing her a towel.

Jill could have told him there was more than one way to accomplish that as she successfully filled his cup and one for herself as well. She had just sat down, a discreet distance from Riordan, when Kerry and Todd returned.

"Ah, coffee!" Todd kneeled beside the pot, wisely picking up the towel before he attempted to pour a cup. "Was that a cougar I heard a while ago?" He directed his question at Riordan as he settled on to the ground near the fire, pulling Kerry down beside him and nestling her in the crook of his arm.

"Yes," Riordan agreed. He caught Jill's startled glance, the glitter in his eyes mocking the fact that she had obviously been deaf to everything when she was in his arms.

"Aren't you going to organize a hunt to go after him?" Todd frowned. "He could raise havoc with the spring calf crop."

"So far he's restricted his prey to the deer. I certainly don't object if he keeps them to a manageable number. That way there aren't so many deer to compete with my cattle for graze. If he shows a taste for beef, I'll have to get rid of him," Riordan shrugged.

Kerry shuddered. "I hope he doesn't."

"So do I," Riordan responded dryly. "As far as I'm concerned, the range is big enough for both of us. I respect the cougar's right to survive. If it's possible I'll drive him out of the area rather than destroy him. That isn't always possible.''

Unwillingly a tightness closed over Jill's throat that Riordan should feel compassion for wild animals and none for humans. Was it his affinity for the land that made him that way?

Later, snuggled in her bedroll, the fire dying beside her, she stared at the stars, the question still unanswered. There was so much about Riordan she under stood. His cynicism, his hardness, his aversion to any lasting relationship with a woman. Yet was there more? Was that little twelve-year-old boy still hiding somewhere inside, sensitive and alone?

The morning sun made Jill forget all her unanswered questions of the night before. The answers were really of little consequence anyway. She was still determined to go ahead with her plans. But she did recognize after last night that it was a dangerous game she was playing, luring Riordan with implied promises she had no intention of fulfilling. It served to make the game more exciting and the vivid color of her eyes revealed it.

While Kerry poured water on the remains of the camp fire, Jill stirred the coals to be certain no live ember remained. Todd was saddling the horses a few yards away and Riordan was loading the packhorse.

"It's all out," Jill announced with a bright smile.

"Last night. . . ." Kerry moved restively, drawing a curious glance from Jill. "Last night, I saw you with Riordan. Jill, what are you doing?" Anxious brown eyes searched Jill's face, as if certain her friend had taken leave of her senses.

"Exactly what it looked like. I was letting Riordan chase me," she replied. Her gaze moved thoughtfully to the broad shoulders of the man in question.

"You know the old saying, Kerry, a boy chases a girl until she catches him. Well, I'm going to catch Riordan."

"Do you mean you've fallen in love with him?" Kerry breathed incredulously.

"No, silly," Jill laughed softly. "I'm not that big a fool. But I think I can get him to agree to your marriage before the month is up. It's impossible to reason with that man. That only leaves female trickery."

"Oh, Jill, do you think you should?"

"Should has nothing to do with it. I'm doing it."

"Come on, honey. We're ready to start back." Todd stood holding the reins to Kerry's horse, effectively ending the conversation between the two.

The mountains in the east were reflecting the purpling pink glow of a setting western sun when the four rode into the ranchyard. During the ride down Jill had not attempted to force a conversation with Riordan or even lightly flirt with him. This was the time to be slightly inaccessible, to be friendly if he made the move but never to imply an intimacy.

One of the ranch hands was there to take the horses. Jill smiled easily when Riordan helped her from the saddle, deliberately ignoring the fraction of a second his hands remained on her waist after she was on the ground.

"I hope Mary has fixed an enormous roast with potatoes and gravy and the works," Todd declared. His arm was nonchalantly draped over Kerry's shoulders as they all started toward the house.

"I hope she's a mind reader and has a hot bubbling tubful of water waiting for us," Jill inserted. "The food can wait."

"You girls can laze in the tub if you want," Todd grinned. "I'll take a quick shower and eat."

"Not all of it. I'm starved, too," Kerry laughed.

"There's a car in the driveway. Oh, oh!" Todd arched a brow expressively at his brother. "It looks like you have a visitor."

Jill recognized the gold and brown car. It belonged to none other than Sheena Benton. This was not exactly the way Jill had wanted to end the day. She slanted a glance at Riordan and caught the watchful glimmer of his gray eyes on her. He expected her to be disappointed.

"Maybe she can stay for dinner," she suggested in a deliberately casual vein.

"I'll ask." Riordan's mouth quirked.

Todd's eyes shifted from one to the other. He had seen what Kerry had seen the night before, and unless Kerry had enlightened him, which Jill doubted, he had put his own construction on it.

"It ought to be an interesting evening," offered Todd dryly. His comment was followed by a sharp dig in his ribs by Kerry's elbow.

Entering the house through the rear door, they found the kitchen empty but with all sorts of delicious smells coming from the oven. In the entrance hall, they could hear Sheena's voice. Jill couldn't make out what she was saying, but it was obvious she was talking to Mary.

"Oh, Riordan, there you are," Sheena declared with purring delight when the foursome walked into the entrance hall.

"Hello, Sheena," Riordan greeted her blandly. "I didn't expect to see you here."

"I was just leaving, actually. Mary told me you'd gone on a trail ride and, of course, I had no idea when you would be back. Did just the four of you go?" Her tiger eyes swerved to Jill, hostility sparkling in their almond shape.

"Just the four of us," Jill answered with a challenging smile.

"It must have been a long ride back. You certainly look grimy and saddlesore," Sheena replied.

Miaow! Jill thought, catching the snapping humor of Mary Rivers's black eyes and trying not to let an answering sparkle enter her own. It would simply not do for Sheena to discover that she and Mary were laughing at her, however silently.

"You're right on both counts," Jill agreed. "Although—" an impish demon made her glance at Riordan "—it was certainly worth it!"

Amber fire flamed over her face and Jill knew she had thoroughly evoked Sheena's jealousy. So did

Riordan. The gray eyes appeared complacently amused.

"What brings you here, Sheena?" he asked. "Business or pleasure?"

"Business mainly." The fires were banked as she swung her gaze to him, the light in her eyes adding that just how much "business" depended on him. "I was hoping I could persuade you to come over one evening and go over my accounts with me."

"Will Friday night be soon enough?" He didn't seem surprised by the request, which led Jill to believe that it was a common one or a smoke screen for a more intimate rendezvous. Or both.

"Friday will be fine," Sheena purred, sending a cool sweeping smile that bordered on triumph to the others in the room. "I'll be going now to leave you all free to wash the trail dust off."

"Aren't you staying for dinner?" Clear blue eyes widened innocently. There was immense satisfaction in turning the tables on Sheena and pretending to be the hostess this time. "I'm sure Mary can stretch the food."

"You're welcome to stay if you like," Riordan inserted, a faint twitch of amusement near one corner of his mouth as if he knew the intent of Jill's invitation.

"Thank you, darling," Sheena purred. "But I know you're all on the verge of collapse. I'll see you Friday "

CHAPTER EIGHT

A BEE MADE a downward swoop toward her head and Jill ducked quickly away from his buzzing path. Raising a hand to shield her eyes from the sun, she looked again to the truck parked beside the fence, its tailgate down. Beyond it and partially hidden by it was Riordan's dark head. Her fingers tightened their grip on the unopened bottle of cold beer.

Since the trail ride, she had seen next to nothing of Riordan. Myriad small obstacles had littered her path, ranging from sick animals to mechanical breakdowns of ranch equipment. Her plans were threatening to stagnate unless she took them in hand. Today was Friday and it was imperative that she make an impression on Riordan before he visited Sheena tonight.

Jill wasn't concerned that given enough time she could overcome the competition presented by the older woman. The problem was she didn't have much time. In a little more than a week, she and Kerry were due to leave.

It had become a case of if the mountain wouldn't come to Mohammed, Mohammed had to go to the mountain. Luckily Riordan was fixing a fence close to the house today, so Mohammed didn't have far to go.

As Jill drew nearer the truck, she ran a hand along the edge of the blouse she had tied around her midriff. There was a light golden quality to the bareness of her waist, courtesy of the hours she and Kerry had lain in the sun. On the surface, the tied blouse was concession to the blazing hot sun overhead, but actually it was intended to draw attention to the slenderness of her waist and suggestive curves of her hips and breasts.

"Hello!" Jill called, hooking a thumb in the loops of her slacks as she rounded the rear of the truck. "Are you working hard?"

Straightening from the fence, Riordan glanced over his shoulder, an odd light flickering briefly in his gray eyes. Jill halted beside the truck, the world spinning crazily for an instant. A naked expanse of bronzed torso glowing with the sheen of perspiration met her eyes. Riordan's shirt lay discarded on the fence post.

"Out for a walk?" There was a substantial degree of cynical mockery in his question.

Leather gloves were pulled off with slow deliberation to join a pair of pliers in one hand as he moved lazily toward the truck and Jill. His gaze slid to the brown-tinted bottle in her hand.

There was a roaring in her ears that she couldn't explain. She gladly shifted her attention to the bottle and away from the hypnotic sight of the tightly curling black hairs on his chest. Good heavens, she'd seen her brothers dressed considerably less decently than that. Why on earth was she letting it disturb her?

"Yes, I was feeling a bit restless and thought I'd walk it off," she admitted, tossing her head back with an air of careless indifference. "Since I had nowhere in particular to go, I thought I'd bring you something cold. The sun is hot today."

"That was thoughtful of you." He leaned against the side of the truck near Jill, laying his gloves and pliers near a roll of barbed wire in the back of the truck before taking the bottle of beer she offered.

"I try to be useful," she smiled, attempting to penetrate the smoky veil of his eyes for some reason behind his dry-voiced response. Riordan could be positively impenetrable at times. This was one of those times.

She watched him unscrew the lid and toss it in back, then lift the bottle to his mouth. As he tilted his head back to drink, she studied the tanned column of his throat, the cords rippling sinewy strong.

Wiping the mouth of the bottle, Riordan offered it to her. "Have a drink. You must be thirsty after your walk."

Her throat did feel a bit dry and tight. Accepting the bottle and raising it to her lips, she could almost feel the warmth of his mouth imprinted on the glass as she took a drink of the malty, cold liquid.

"Where's Kerry?" Riordan asked, his fingers accidentally—or on purpose—touching Jill's as he took the bottle from her hand.

"At the house." *Still insisting that I'm out of my mind for attempting such a thing,* Jill added to herself.

An uneasiness settled over her. She glanced away from Riordan, pretending an interest in the distant mountains sculptured against a wide blue sky. The gray eyes watched silently, leaving her with the unshakable feeling that it had been a mistake to come out here.

"I suppose I ought to let you get back to your work," she offered, for want of anything better to say.

"Not yet," Riordan drawled complacently.

Jill glanced in surprise at the wrist that was suddenly a firm captive of his hand. "I . . . only came to bring you something to drink. Mary thought you might like a cold beer."

"Mary thought?" A brow arched quizzically, a dark glitter laughing at her in his eyes. "She must be getting forgetful, otherwise she would have remembered the cooler of beer she sent with me at noon."

Damn! Why had she allowed herself to be tripped up in her own lie? That was a teenager's mistake.

"Maybe that's what she said and I misunderstood her," she bluffed. "In either case, I'm keeping you from your work."

"I'm not objecting."

The bottle was set half-full inside the truck. Applying pressure to her wrist, Riordan drew her toward him. Short of struggling Jill couldn't resist.

The initiative of any embrace was supposed to have been at her invitation and not this soon. She let her legs carry her reluctantly toward him, almost sighing in relief when he let her stop a scant foot from him. At the moment her senses were clamoring too loudly at his nearness. She needed a few seconds to regain her sense of objectivity before coming in physical contact with him.

His superior height forced her to tilt her head back to meet his hooded arrogant gaze. "Riordan, I—"

A hand touched her cheek, halting her words as effectively as if it had covered her mouth. "How many men have told you that your eyes are the color of the sky?" he mused cynically. "A Montana sky, vivid blue and pulling a man into the promise of heaven beyond."

No sooner was Jill aware of her wrist being released then she felt his hand on the bare flesh of her waist. The strong male scent of him was an erotic stimulus she didn't want to feel.

"Please!" Her effort to appear indifferent was thwarted by the involuntary catch in her voice.

"Didn't you wander into this meadow with the intention of bestowing some of the honey from your lips on me, butterfly?" Riordan taunted.

A tiny gasp parted her lips. His hand curved around the back of her neck, drawing her upward to his mouth. The naked chest was satiny smooth and sensual beneath her fingers, hard muscles flexing as he molded her against him. Her lips moved in response to his to deepen the kiss until a wild, glorious song burst in her heart.

The melody raced through her veins. Jill was only half aware of Riordan pressing her backward. Spiky blades of grass scratched her bare back as his weight pinned her to the ground. The caress of his hands was arousing, exhorting her to give—and to plead with her body to receive—more in return.

The tails of her blouse were untied and the buttons

undone with careless ease. Her nipple hardened under his touch and she moaned in surrender. The reason she had come was completely lost under the spell of ecstasy flaming through her.

When his head raised from hers, she locked her arms around his neck to draw him back. His fingers closed over her wrists and firmly pulled her hands away, his mouth twisting harshly.

"Sorry, butterfly. I'm not satisfied either, but we are about to have company," Riordan mocked the glaze of desire in her eyes.

Rolling to his feet, he stood above her. Dominated as she was by raging primitive emotions, it took a full second for Jill to realize the significance of what he had said. The sound of a car engine could be heard crossing the meadow and drawing nearer. She scrambled to her feet, cheeks flaming at her complete lack of control, and turned away from his taunting gaze to hastily button her blouse.

The task was barely completed by her shaking hands when the car stopped beside the truck. Self-consciously brushing golden hair away from her face, Jill turned. She wanted to scream in frustration at the sight of Sheena Benton.

"Am I interrupting something, Riordan?" Sheena drawled archly, leaning against the steering wheel of her car, fingers curling like unsheathed claws over the wheel.

"It'll keep," Riordan shrugged, slanting a mocking glance at Jill's still flushed cheeks. "What can I do for you?"

"I wanted to remind you about tonight." Her statement was directed at Riordan, but the hatred in her eyes was solely for Jill.

"I hadn't forgotten," Riordan assured her smoothly, an intimate dark light entering his eyes.

"If you can get away, why not come early?" Sheena suggested. A purring entered her voice at his look. "You can check the accounts over dinner."

"I should be able to arrange that," he agreed aloofly, and was rewarded with a dazzling smile. Nausea churned Jill's stomach.

"I won't keep you," Sheena murmured, shifting the car into gear and glancing with feline archness to Jill. "Can I give you a lift to the house, Jill?"

"No, thank you," she retorted coldly. "I prefer to walk."

The coral red mouth tightened with displeasure. "Suit yourself," Sheena clipped with a toss of her chestnut mane. Blowing a kiss to Riordan, she reversed to turn back the way she had come.

"Are you going back now?" Riordan asked with insinuating softness.

"Yes," Jill answered decisively, wishing the heat in her cheeks would ease. "Right away."

"I would suggest before you get back to the house to fix your blouse," he jeered. "You've buttoned it crooked."

A mortified glance at the front of her blouse confirmed his statement. There was not the slightest chance that the sharp-eyed Sheena had not noticed it.

"Thanks, I'll do that," Jill retorted defiantly, refusing to show any guilt about her action.

But guilt hounded her steps all the way back to the house. She had intended to entrap Riordan with his physical attraction for her. Despite the way he had aroused her in previous encounters with his lovemaking, she had never expected he would awaken her inner desires and the extent of her womanhood. In all honesty, her confidence was badly shaken.

Riordan wasn't at the dinner table when she entered the dining room with Kerry and Todd. She left it to Mary Rivers to explain where he was. There was a noticeable lack of desire to mention her meeting with Riordan that afternoon and she avoided the questing look from Mary.

The perfectly prepared meal was utterly tasteless, but Jill forced down nearly everything on her plate. She didn't want to parry any questions about a lack of appetite. After the meal, she retreated to a corner of the living room with a book, ostensibly affording Kerry and Todd some privacy.

Her thoughts were as jumbled and confused as they had been earlier. The printed lines on the book page blurred. She simply couldn't concentrate . . . on anything. The only thing that seemed to register was the portrait of the copper-haired woman with sparkling hazel eyes that hung above the mantelpiece. A butterfly like herself.

Suddenly restless, Jill snapped the book in her lap shut, drawing startled glances from Todd and Kerry.

"I think I'll go and see if Mary needs some help in the kitchen," she said in explanation.

But the kitchen was sparkling clean and the house-keeper was nowhere to be seen. With the half-formed idea to take a walk outside, Jill wandered down the back hall towards the rear entrance.

A closed door drew her hypnotically. She knew it was Riordan's room. Mary had mentioned it one day in passing, but Jill had never been inside. Curiosity surged to the forefront, a sudden need filling her to see his room.

Cautiously she opened the door and walked into the room, touching the light switch. The small light over-head left the corners of the room in shadows. Jill stared silently around her, taking in the single bed against one side of a wall with a small table beside it and the chest of drawers against another wall. A rigid, straight-backed chair occupied one corner.

Compared to the quiet elegance of the rest of the house, the stark simplicity of this room was unexpected. It was almost monastic. Very quietly Jill closed the door behind her, aware that she was trespassing but unable to leave.

Riordan was a man of basics. She had always guessed that. Yet, walking to the single bed, she couldn't stop wondering why he had chosen to shun the more luxurious creature comforts offered by the rest of the house for this. Did he need to sleep here to remain hard and cynical? Was he avoiding the gentle, feminine touches she had noticed in the rest of the house?

Fingering the agricultural book on the bedside table, Jill smiled at herself. She was crazy to come in here. The room revealed no more about Riordan than he did himself. She was being overly imaginative to believe otherwise.

A striped Hudson Bay blanket covered the bed. Without being consciously aware of what she was doing, Jill sat down on the edge of the bed. The mattress was firm without being rock hard, a fact she noticed absently as she gazed about the room.

A movement caught her eye, and freezing with cold dread, she saw the doorknob turning. She couldn't breathe and as the door opened, she offered a hurried prayer that it would be Mary Rivers she saw. It was much too early for Riordan to come back.

But it was his broad-shouldered lean-hipped frame that filled the opening. Gray eyes met the startled roundness of her blue ones. Jill's heart was in her throat. She couldn't think of one legitimate reason she could offer as an excuse for her presence in his room. With a speculative glitter, his gaze swept over her.

"This is an unexpected invitation," Riordan murmured dryly, stepping into the room and closing the door.

Heat flamed through her cheeks as Jill suddenly realized she was sitting on his bed. She rose hurriedly to her feet.

The hard line of his mouth quirked mockingly. "There's no need to get up. I would have joined you."

"I . . . I was just going," Jill stammered.

"You don't need to slip into something more comfortable." His steel gray eyes studied her with lazy intensity, lingering on the trembling parting of her mouth, the pulsing vein in her neck and finally the vee of her blouse.

Her hand protectively covered the vee. "You don't understand," she protested nervously. "I didn't expect you back so soon. I thought you . . . I mean, Sheena. . . ." There simply wasn't any way she could put into words exactly what she thought he and Sheena would be doing.

"After this afternoon, did you honestly think I would prefer the scratching of a jealous cat when I could have the fluttering softness of a butterfly?" Teeth flashed white with his wolfish smile as he took a step toward her.

"No!" Her breath was fast and uneven. "I know what you must be thinking, finding me in your room and all," she rushed wildly. "I only came in because I was curious." The grooves around his mouth deepened. "It's not at all what you're thinking, I swear."

"Don't bother to bat those innocent blue eyes at me," he taunted. "Or deny that your visit this afternoon was designed to implant your image in my mind when I went to see Sheena tonight. You were maneuvering again, Jill. We both know it."

She opened her mouth to try to protest the truth of his statement. It would be futile. There were too many disturbing emotions stirring inside her for her to lie convincingly.

"Excuse me, but I really must go," she murmured

unsteadily, keeping her eyes downcast as she started toward the door.

"Now what's the game?" Riordan was in her way, blocking the path to the door. "Are you playing hard to get?"

"I'm not playing anything. Please let me by. There was room to pass him, but Jill didn't trust him.

"I see." He was laughing at her, silently, but the cynical amusement was in his eyes. "You simply flitted into my room by accident, drawn only by curiosity. Now you want to fly away, is that it, leaving me with the teasing picture of you waiting on my bed."

"Riordan, please!" Jill swallowed tightly.

Trading words with him was useless. She had to escape before she became enmeshed in the backlash of her plans. At this moment she was too unprepared to cope with Riordan or her wayward reactions to him.

On legs quaking like aspen leaves, she started for the door. As she drew level with him, she held her breath, flinching when his hand moved. But it didn't reach out for her. Instead it snapped off the overhead light, throwing the room into darkness.

Stopped by the unexpectedness of his action and her own momentary blindness, Jill wasn't able to move. The suggestive intimacy of the bedroom, isolated from the living area of the house, washed over her like shockwaves.

"Once you trap a butterfly—" his low voice was closer, a soft and seductive weapon, and she gasped at his hands gripped her shoulders "—you must take it by the wings."

"Let me go!" she cried breathlessly, frightened by her sudden desire to lean submissively against his chest. She tried to wrench free of his grip, but Riordan used her twisting motion to pivot her around, easily drawing her unbalanced body against his.

His dark head bent and he brushed his mouth against the sensitive skin below her right ear. Jill couldn't control the shudder of delight. The heady male scent of him enveloped her, earthy and clean. Tilting her head to one side, she tried to elude his provocative caress, but only succeeded in exposing more of her neck to his exploring mouth.

"No," she pleaded, shaking back the feathery length of her gold hair and increasing the pressure of her hands that strained against his chest.

Riordan laughed softly, a deep delicious sound that shivered down her spine. His mouth lifted to the averted line of her jaw.

"Isn't this the way you planned it, Jill?" he taunted. His warm breath fanned across the already hot skin of her cheek.

"I didn't plan this," she protested in a desperate whisper. Her eyes were beginning to adjust to the softness of the starlight streaming through the windows.

"You didn't *plan* to make me want you?" Riordan jeered. Jill breathed in sharply. "I know you did. The idea has been in the back of your mind since the first time we met. Everything you've done has been calculated to blind me with desire for you so you could twist me around your finger, take what you wanted and fly away.''

"No," Jill gulped.

She bent her head backward, trying again to escape the disturbing nearness of his mouth. Strong fingers spread across the small of her back, molding her arching body more fully against the male vigor of his. A dizzying weakness spread through her limbs. Her tightly closed lashes fluttered open, focusing her gaze on his rugged features. Half-closed eyes studied her upturned face with a silvery fire that stole her breath.

"You look like some pagan goddess," Riordan murmured deeply, "with that passionate mouth and those eyes sparkling with starfire."

"Please!" she begged to be released.

A hand curled its fingers in the long silken hair at the back of her neck. Jill knew his mouth would tantalize her lips no longer and she started to struggle against the inevitable. But the hand on her neck wouldn't allow her to avoid his kiss. Her hammering fists glanced harmlessly off his chest and shoulders.

At last his conquering mouth had her fingers curling into the thin material of his shirt, clinging to him weakly in surrender. Riordan wasn't content with submission as he parted her lips with persuasive mastery, exploring her mouth until Jill responded with demanding hunger.

Reason was banished completely under the molding caress of his hands. There was only the whirling, mindless ecstasy of his embrace urging her to new heights of sensual awareness. She was achingly conscious of her need for physical gratification, and the hard maleness of Riordan made her aware of his.

The trailing fire of his lips burned over her eyes, cheek and throat, branding her as his possession, and she didn't deny it. Her hands were around his neck, fingers winding into the thick blackness of his hair. His hard mouth closed again over hers, uniting their flames into a roaring fire of passion that sang in her ears.

Like a drowning person, Jill made one last attempt to be saved when his mouth blazed a path to the hollow of her throat.

"I can't—"

Her thoughts were too chaotic. What couldn't she do? She couldn't stop. She couldn't think. She couldn't breathe. She couldn't exist without the wildfire of his touch.

"I'm insane," she ended with a sighing groan.

His head lifted briefly, fingers sliding to her throat. "That's the way I want you to be," Riordan muttered harshly. "Driven to madness until you can think of nothing else but me." He spoke against her lips, his mouth moving mobilely over them in a caress that was designed to make her ache for his kiss. "I want your wings to be singed so you can't fly away until sunrise."

Jill breathed in sharply, knowing she didn't ever want to fly away yet realizing how dangerous it would be to give in to her emotions so completely.

"Kerry . . . Todd . . . " she offered in protest.

Riordan's mouth shut off her words until she stopped caring about Kerry and Todd. Only then did he answer.

"They'll be enjoying the privacy you've been so keen for them to have. They won't miss you. I doubt if Todd even expected me back tonight."

Weakly Jill shook her head, but unable to deny the truth of what he said. Lowering her head, she felt his lips against her hair, their moistness tangling in the silken gold.

"Riordan, I—"

The support of his hard masculine body was taken away from her and she swayed toward him. Her movement was checked as an arm slid under her knees and she was lifted into the air, cradled against his chest. Automatically her hands circled his neck.

As he turned toward the small bed, a shaft of starlight glittered over his face. The strength of purpose stamped in the forceful, handsome lines caught at Jill's throat. Nothing could stop him. The same primitive mood had her in its spell and she knew she didn't want to try to prevent what seemed so inevitable and paradoxically so right.

Sitting on the side of the bed, Riordan held her on his lap. His face was in shadows, but she knew the gray eyes were studying her. This was her last chance to protest. Instead her fingers began exploring the blunt angles of his features, feather soft and caressing.

He seemed to be prolonging the moment when he claimed her as if to make the possession sweeter. Feeling wantonly bold, Jill leaned forward and pressed her lips against his mouth. It curved briefly under her touch into a complacent smile.

"The bed isn't made for two," Riordan murmured huskily, the grooves around his mouth deepening in satisfaction, "but tonight I don't think either one of us will care."

An almost inaudible moan of complete surrender slipped from her throat as Riordan bent her backward onto the mattress. His hand slid intimately from her thigh to her hip and along to the curve of her breast. The pressing weight of his male body followed her down, his mouth unerringly and possessively finding hers. Jill was lost in an erotic dreamworld of sensations that she never wanted to end. She succumbed with rapturous delight to each new touch.

"Jill?" A familiar voice was trying to enter her dream. Jill's head moved in protest to its call. "Jill? Where are you?"

"No!" she gave a muffled cry to forbid the entry.

"Sssh." Riordan's strong fingers lightly covered her mouth. His indirect acknowledgment of the voice that called her made the dreamworld begin to fade into reality.

"Jill?" Now she could recognize the voice as Kerry's, still distant but moving closer. "Where could she be?"

"She did say she was going to the kitchen, didn't she?" Todd was with Kerry.

"Yes, but she isn't here," came the muffled reply of concern.

Reason and sanity came back with shocking swiftness as Jill tried to twist from beneath Riordan's weight. He checked the movement easily.

"No," his low voice commanded near her ear. "You know you don't really want to leave."

"Yes . . . no." The conflicting answers were crazily the truth as Jill was torn in two by her emotions.

"Maybe she went outside for a walk," Todd suggested.

"It isn't like her not to tell me. Oh, Todd, let's check." Kerry rushed, and footsteps started down the hall that led past Riordan's room to the rear door of the house.

Jill's hands pushed frantically against the stone wall of his chest. "They'll find us," she whispered desperately.

His warm breath moved over her cheek in silent laughter. "They won't look for you in here," he mocked, his mouth following the curve of her throat to the tantalizing hollow between her breasts.

"N-n-no!" Her protest was shaken by the violent surge of desire brought on by his intimate touch.

"She could have gone up to her room, too," Todd said as the two sets of footsteps walked by the bedroom door.

"Let's check outside first," Kerry replied anxiously.

"She's a grown woman. She can take care of—" The "herself" was lost as the closing back door cut off the rest of Todd's statement.

"I told you they wouldn't find us," Riordan murmured against her skin.

"B-but they'll keep on looking," Jill moaned softly,

her hands still straining against him. "Please let me go."

"No." His fingers closed over her chin, holding it motionless as his mouth closed over hers in a drugging kiss that sent her floating nearly all the way back into her dreamworld.

The click of the bedroom doorknob splintered through her. The alert tensing of Riordan's muscles told her he had heard it too, but he didn't lift his mouth from hers nor allow her protesting lips to twist away.

"Riordan, they're looking for her." Mary Rivers spoke from the doorway.

His hold relaxed slightly as he raised his head, his gaze glittering, holding Jill's pleading blue eyes. Hot waves of shame licked through her veins.

"Get out of here, Mary," Riordan ordered smoothly.

Tearing her eyes from his face, Jill twisted her head toward the housekeeper, her tall stocky build outlined by the light streaming into the room from the hallway. Her throat worked convulsively, but nothing came out. Part of her didn't want to be rescued.

"You can't do it, Riordan," Mary sighed, but with firm conviction.

"Can't I?" he jeered arrogantly. "The lady is more than willing," he added with sarcastic emphasis.

"Let her go."

He smiled coolly down at Jill. "She's free to leave," he rolled away from her, only a hand remaining spread on her stomach as a wicked gray light held her gaze captive, "*if* she really wants to leave."

Perhaps if he hadn't been so confident she would stay or if he had asked her not to leave him, Jill would have remained where she was. Instead, with a frightened sob at what a fool she had nearly made of herself, she scrambled to her feet.

Two wavering steps toward the door were all she had taken before the soft flesh of her upper arms was seized in a biting grip. Weakly she allowed herself to be pulled back against his chest, her head lolling against his shoulder, unable to deny the disturbance his touch caused.

"Riordan," Mary warned swiftly.

"No, she can go," he interrupted in an ominously low voice laced with contempt. "She and I both know that I wasn't seducing her. She was letting me seduce her. Almost since the day she came, she's been inviting me to make love to her, deliberately holding back so she could twist me around her finger. She knew I found her as physically attractive as any man would and she intended to use that attraction to get what she wanted. Isn't that right, Jill?" he demanded savagely.

She didn't have the strength to disagree even if he was wrong, but he wasn't wrong and she didn't argue. "Yes, yes, that's right," she admitted in a breathy whisper.

"But I'm not twisted around your finger." The derisive jeer slashed at her pride. "I take what I want and when I'm through with it, I throw it away." He released her with a slight push toward the door and

Mary. "You can go. But I'm not quite through with you yet."

With that half-threat and half-promise ringing in the air, Jill stumbled forward. Mary wrapped a supporting arm around her shoulders and led her from the room. Drained of all emotion except the cold feeling of dread, Jill was barely aware of the housekeeper's presence.

"I'll take you upstairs to your room," said Mary.

Jill was suddenly conscious of how disheveled she must look. Her clothes were in a revealing state of disarray and her lips had to be swollen from his passionate kisses. She knew she had the look of a woman who had been made love to. A sob strangled her throat. She very nearly had!

She cast a surreptitious glance at the housekeeper, wondering what this proud woman thought of her. The only part of Riordan's accusation that had been a lie was when he had suggested that she had intended that he seduce her. Jill had never contemplated going that far, but she had set out to twist him around her finger. She had planned to make Riordan want her so badly he would do anything.

When they reached her bedroom, Jill caught the look of gentle compassion in Mary's dark eyes. In shame and humiliation, she knew guiltily that she didn't deserve the woman's understanding.

"I'm all right," Jill asserted forcefully, averting her face from the housekeeper's concerned gaze. Her legs now strong enough to deny the need for a supporting arm, Jill stepped forward. "Would you tell Kerry that you saw me and that . . . that I have a headache and have gone to my room?''

"I'll see that you're not disturbed," Mary nodded perceptively, "by anyone."

By anyone, Jill knew she meant Riordan, too. And she didn't doubt that the woman would figuratively stand guard at her door. When Mary left, Jill buried her face in her hands, but she didn't cry.

Hysterical laughter sobbed in her throat. She barely smothered it with her hand. The irony of the situation struck her forcibly. All along she had believed Riordan was chasing her. Instead, she had been chasing him and he had caught her. She was the one who had been brought to her knees.

Never once in all her planning had she ever seriously considered the possibility that she might fall in love with Riordan. Yet that was exactly what she had done. She knew it as clearly and as certainly as she knew her own name.

Tonight had not been the result of a sudden desire for physical experience or the arousing attention of an experienced lover. They were a potent combination but not an explanation for her complete abandonment of reason. Love was the answer, no matter how foolish and painful the emotion might be.

CHAPTER NINE

JILL STARED at the rising golden globe on the eastern horizon. Blue eyes were glazed with pain, faint etchings of red at the corners. Not from tears. She hadn't cried. Not a single tear had come forward to ease the ache in her heart.

The redness was from exhaustion. She had not slept. She had not even attempted to sleep nor made the pretense that she would. Still dressed in the same clothes, she had alternately paced the room and stared sightlessly out the window. Sometimes she thought of nothing except what it had been like in Riordan's arms. At other times, her mind raced wildly to come up with a scheme to make Riordan love her. All were rejected eventually. He would see through them just as he had seen through all of her other maneuvers.

There was a subdued knock at her door, and she spun from the window. It couldn't be Kerry. She would use the connecting door. Todd was out of the question. Mary?

"W-who is it?" she called shakily.

"Riordan," was the low response.

A shaft of pure joy pierced her heart. She wanted to

race to the door, fling it open and throw herself into his arms. She jammed a fist in her mouth.

"Go away," she said tightly, biting into her knuckles.

The doorknob turned, but for some unknown reason Jill had locked it last night. Now she bowed her head in thankfulness.

"A locked door isn't going to stop me, Jill. Open it!"

It wasn't an idle threat. Still, she hesitated before walking over and turning the key in the lock. Control was the key, she told herself as she walked quickly away. She had to remain calm and controlled. She mustn't let her emotions surface, nor the love she felt for him.

Again at the window, she halted. He was in the room, the door closed behind him. Jill stared sightlessly out of the window.

"What do you want?" she demanded.

"If you had trouble sleeping last night, why didn't you come downstairs?"

Jill glanced sharply over her shoulder just as Riordan turned away from the bed that bore not the slightest imprint of having been slept in. Aloof gray eyes caught her look and held it, a cynical quirk to his hard mouth.

"Leave me alone, Riordan," she snapped harshly at his arrogant expression, then breathed in deeply to regain the control she needed so desperately. Yet it seemed that the only way she had of concealing her love for him was to lash out with anger.

"Not yet," he answered with cold mockery. "I've come to tell you that you can move your things down to my room this morning. I'll have a larger bed and another chest of drawers moved in."

Slowly Jill turned from the window, her head tipped to one side in disbelief. "What?" she breathed incredulously.

A brow arched higher. "I thought I'd made it clear. I'm not the type to go sneaking around and taking part in midnight rendezvous."

"So you're simply arranging for me to sleep with you?" Her hands moved to a challenging position on her hips.

"Spare me the pretense of indignation." His mouth moved into a crooked, jeering line. "I'm sure your friend Kerry is aware of the facts of life. No doubt she'll find it romantic and excitingly risqué. If you prefer, I'll explain to her and Todd."

"And what will you explain? That I'm your new sleeping partner, your lover, your mistress?" Jill demanded coldly. "I would be curious to know exactly what position you're offering me."

The dark head was tipped arrogantly back, the gray eyes clear and piercing like an eagle's. "Whatever label suits you," replied Riordan.

"What is the duration of this position?" A cold sarcasm filled her heart and, momentarily at least, eased the pain. "Until you're through with me?"

"I'm not setting any time limit, butterfly." There was faint contempt in his tone. "Whichever one of us tires of the other first can call it quits."

"I see," she said tautly. "And you expect me to fall all over myself accepting this arrangement?"

Riordan moved slowly to stand in front of her and it was all Jill could do to hold her ground and not retreat. He towered over her for a long moment.

His hand reached out to touch the petal softness of her cheek. Something melted inside her at his caress and she had to steel herself not to visibly react.

"You were eager enough for me to make love to you last night," Riordan reminded her softly.

The peculiar light in his eyes made her heart skip a beat. Yet the indecision of what to do that had plagued her all night was gone. Under these circumstances, there was only one thing she could do.

"Yes," she admitted calmly, "I did want you to make love to me last night."

There was a satisfied movement of his mouth. "Do you want me to send Mary up to help you pack your things?"

Jill moved away from the hand that was still resting on her cheek and walked to the center of the room. She clasped her hands in front of her, staring at her twining fingers for an instant before she tossed her head back and met his alert gaze.

"Please do send Mary." A chilling calm spread over her. "I would like to pack and get out of this house as soon as possible."

The room crackled with a stunned silence. His gaze narrowed fractionally, followed by a short sardonically amused sigh.

"Are you flying away already, butterfly?" There

was an indifferent movement of his mouth. "Even that was too much of a commitment for you to make?"

His aloof comment stung. If he had indicated in any way that he cared for her, Jill would have willingly committed her life to him. She felt the moistness of tears on her lashes.

"There is one more thing," she squeezed the words out through the lump in her throat, "before I ask you to leave my room. I want you to give your approval of Todd's marriage to Kerry."

Again he walked to stand in front of her, not touching her this time, as his glaze focused on a crystal drop threatening to fall from a dark gold lash.

"Tears?" Riordan jeered. "That must be the oldest female maneuver in the book. You must be digging deep in your bag of tricks to come up with that one!"

Jill stared at her hands, unable to meet his satirical look. "I don't doubt that you find them amusing. I don't think you're capable of feeling anything but your own primitive needs." She took a deep breath, not raising her eyes. "You don't know your brother very well either, because if you did, you would know he's capable of very deep feelings. He cares about you, but he'll only allow you to stand in the way of his happiness for a short while. You can threaten him with money or any other thing you want, but in the end he will marry Kerry and hate you. Maybe you don't care. Family probably means nothing to you. If it doesn't, then it can't matter what Todd does with his life."

"Are you finished interfering?" Riordan snapped.

"Yes." Jill turned away, her shoulders slightly hunched forward, a terrible coldness in her heart. "Will you go now? And . . . And I would prefer not to see you again before I leave."

"That makes two of us," he agreed mockingly.

The bedroom door slammed and another tear slipped from her lashes. Jill wiped it determinedly away. She wasn't going to cry, not when she knew she was doing the only thing possible. She walked to the closet and started yanking out her clothes. A few minutes later Mary was there, silently helping her, not needing the reason for Jill's sudden departure explained.

The last suitcase had been snapped shut when there was a knock on her door. Jill couldn't move, terrified that it might be Riordan and her resolve to leave would crumble if she had to be near him again. But when Mary opened the door, it was Todd who stood in the hallway.

"Riordan said that as soon as you were ready I'm supposed to take you home," he said quietly. "He said you had an argument." But his hazel eyes said he knew it was more complicated than that.

"Yes . . . well," she ran a shaking hand over her forehead, "I'm ready." She glanced hesitantly toward the connecting door to Kerry's room.

"I'll explain to Kerry if you'd like to leave now," Todd offered.

She darted him a grateful look. "Thank you, Todd. And you, too, Mary." She gave the housekeeper a quick hug before picking up one of the smaller cases and hurrying toward the door.

With the rest of her luggage under his arm, Todd started to follow, then glanced back at Mary. "When Kerry wakes up...."

The housekeeper smiled gently. "I'll tell her you'll explain everything when you get back."

BUTTERFLIES COULD FLY AWAY and never look back. Jill didn't feel very much like a butterfly. She doubted if she ever would again.

Taking her foot off the accelerator, she gently applied the brakes to ease the car around the curve in the snow-packed road. The Christmas-wrapped packages on the seat started to slip and she put out a hand to stop them. She didn't feel in the holiday spirit either. She just hoped that once she was home with her parents and brothers and sisters, she would catch the festive mood.

After the way she had moped around the house this past summer when she had left the ranch, her parents were entitled to expect some improvement in her disposition. They had been wonderfully understanding, although they couldn't really believe there was a man who wouldn't love their daughter. Of course, Jill hadn't told them the whole story. Kerry was the only one who came close to knowing all of it.

The car she was driving had been a consoling gesture from her parents. They had shrugged it off by saying that they were tired of making double trips back and forth to Helena to pick her up on the holiday vacations. They would not be too pleased, though, when they discovered she had made this trip without Kerry's company.

Her engagement to Todd was still on, even though Todd had transferred to Harvard and Kerry had remained in Helena. They had made the decision not to marry until Kerry had finished college, even though it meant a separation. Jill had never had the courage to inquire whether the waiting period had been Riordan's idea, although she had guessed that it was. His name was never mentioned unless by Jill.

Todd had flown back from Harvard to spend Christmas with Kerry. Jill had invited both of them to come home with her, but Todd had declined. He wanted to be certain to catch his flight back. With the unpredictability of winter storms, he didn't object to being snowbound at the airport as long as he wasn't stranded two hundred miles away from it. Naturally Kerry preferred to stay in Helena with him, especially after he had given her his mother's engagement ring.

Jill touched the beige tan cameo suspended by a delicate gold chain around her neck, Todd's Christmas present to her. It, too, had belonged to his mother—she remembered how startled she had been when he told her that. She had held it for long minutes, unwilling to put it around her neck.

"Does Riordan know you gave me this?" she had asked finally. A cold hand had closed over her heart to keep it from beating.

Shortly after Todd had arrived in Helena, he had

driven to the ranch to see his brother and to select
Kerry's engagement ring from his mother's jewelry.

"Yes, he knows," Todd had answered quietly. His
eyes had examined Jill's frozen expression. "After I'd
taken Kerry's ring from the box, I mentioned that I
wanted to buy a gift, so Riordan told me to pick out
something I thought you might like from Mother's
jewelry."

Jill had forced a bright smile onto her taut lips. "It's
very lovely, and I do like it," she said, fastening the
cameo necklace around her neck. "Are you and Kerry
driving out to the ranch for Christmas day?"

"No, Jill, Kerry and I want a peaceful Christmas,"
he had said with decided emphasis.

"I'm sure Sheena will keep him company," Jill had
shrugged, but a shaft of jealousy had drilled deep.

"She's gone to Palm Springs for the holidays. She
came to see Riordan while I was there," Todd had
explained.

Later Jill had summoned the courage to ask if
Riordan had given his approval of their engagement.
It had seemed likely since Riordan had evidently
permitted Todd to give Kerry their mother's ring.

Todd had breathed in deeply, a slightly closed look
stealing into his expression. "Let's just say that he's
reconciled to the fact that he can't change my mind."

Sighing heavily, Jill couldn't help wondering if
Riordan hadn't relaxed his opposition to their engagement just a little bit. He might not have given his
wholehearted approval, but at least he was not taking
such a hard line against it.

And the necklace she wore, did it have any special significance? Was it an indirect and private way of apologizing? Whoever said that hope sprang eternal certainly was right, Jill thought wryly. Here she was hoping for a miracle. Of course, Christmas is a miracle time, she reminded herself, so maybe it was only natural.

Christmas. It was a time for family gatherings and enormous dinners. Jill could visualize her own home with holly strung on evergreen branches all through the living room, dining room and hall. Her father would have mistletoe hung in every archway and from every light fixture. And her mother would have the stockings they had used as children hung over the fireplace, waiting for Santa.

The tree would be gigantic, covered with tinsel, angel hair, and the ornaments that had become old friends over the years. Plates of Christmas candy and bowls of colored popcorn balls would be all over the house, promising an extra five pounds of weight to anyone who dared to touch them. Logs would be in readiness in the fireplace, but a fire wouldn't be started until Christmas morning, after Santa Claus had safely made his visit.

That was Christmas to Jill.

Unbidden the question came—what was Christmas to Riordan? Todd had told her Riordan was in his teens when he had stopped accompanying his father to Helena to spend Christmas with his mother. How many lonely Christmasses had he spent in that big house without family and with only Mary Rivers as company? No family and probably no decorations. Men didn't take the time to do such things on their own, and what would there have been to celebrate?

And what about that little twelve-year-old boy who had been forced to shoot his horse when it had broken its legs? That little boy who had grown into a man, a man who wouldn't give horses names in case he had to destroy one again. That same man was spending Christmas alone again this year. His own brother had chosen the company of the woman he loved over Riordan, just as their father had done.

Suddenly it didn't matter whether Todd's decision was warranted or not. It just seemed so totally unfair that Riordan was going to be alone again.

Jill turned into the first plowed side road she found and reversed her direction back the way she had come. A couple of miles back she had passed the crossroads intersection and the highway that would take her to the Riordan ranch. One of the packages on the seat contained a sweater for her father. With luck, it would fit Riordan. Another contained a handcrafted shawl she could give Mary.

His present would be a conciliatory gesture on her part. He might just meet her halfway. There was that eternal hope again! She smiled sadly. More than likely, Riordan would think it was another trick she was playing, a maneuver of some sort. But she didn't care. She simply had to see him.

The lane leading from the cleared county road to the ranch house had not been plowed. Several sets of tracks ran over each other in the general direction of the buildings located on the other side of the meadow, presently out of sight behind the rise. Jill offered a silent prayer that she wouldn't get stuck as the car crunched over the tire-packed snow.

The winter sun set early in the north country. It was barely past mid-afternoon and already there was a purpling pink cast to the snow-covered mountains. Jill refused to think about the rest of her drive home in the dark.

The house, nestled in the protective stand of snow-draped evergreens, looked somehow bigger and emptier than she remembered. A tense excitement gripped her as she selected the packages from the rest and stepped out of the car.

At the front door, she hesitated, gathering her courage before she opened the door. Maybe it was a subconscious wish to catch Riordan unawares that had prompted her to enter without knocking, or maybe she had become accustomed to simply walking in after spending those fateful weeks in the house that summer.

The house was silently empty. A fire crackling in the entryway hearth would have made the house seem warm, but there was none. Slipping off her snowboots, Jill listened attentively for some sound of human occupation.

It suddenly occurred to her that Riordan might not even be here. He could be at one of the barns or at another section of the ranch altogether. That would only leave Mary Rivers. She would undoubtedly be in the kitchen. Jill slowly exhaled the breath she had been unconsciously holding. It was probably just as well that she hadn't seen Riordan, she decided, but she would speak to Mary.

The awesome silence of the house had her tiptoeing on the hardwood floor of the hall leading to the kitchen in the rear. As she drew closer, she caught the aroma of cooking and smiled. Mary was there.

Her hand was on the kitchen doorknob ready to turn it to open the door when she heard Riordan's voice come from inside the kitchen.

"I don't care what you're fixing. I told you I'm not hungry," he snapped.

"Then have some coffee and stop grouching about like a grizzly," Mary replied evenly.

"I am not grouching," Riordan answered tightly.

"Snapping my head off every five minutes is not grouching?" the housekeeper inquired dryly. "You either have a severe case of cabin fever or you're thinking about that girl. Which is it?"

Jill held her breath, unable to move until Riordan had answered. There was a heavy silence before he spoke in a cuttingly indifferent voice.

"What girl?"

"Jill, of course, as if you didn't know."

"I wasn't thinking of her," Riordan replied.

"Weren't you?" Mary countered. "When are you going to give up and ask the girl to marry you?"

Jill's heart exploded against her rib cage, pounding so fiercely it seemed impossible they couldn't hear it.

There was a sudden scrape of a chair leg. "That

would be the height of absurdity!'' he jeered. The pounding of her heart stopped almost abruptly.

"Why?"

"You know why, Mary," Riordan sighed angrily. His cryptic statement was followed by a long pause as though he was waiting for the housekeeper to comment. Bitterness and contempt coated his next words. "I remember one August when mother made one of her unexpected departures. I was thirteen or fourteen at the time. Dad came in the house after saying goodbye to her, looking all hollow and beaten. I demanded that he go and get her and make her stay with us, but he said he couldn't use force to keep her or beg or bribe her to stay. The only thing he could do, he said, was to simply love her."

"He was right, Riordan," Mary agreed quietly.

"Right!" he returned with a scoffing laugh. "In all the times she left him, I never saw dad cry once—only when she died. Then he became half a man. When she was alive, you know how many winter evenings he sat in front of her portrait and how impossible it was to get him to leave that room when she died. No woman has a right to bring a man down like that. He was strong and intelligent, a giant, and she had no right to make a fool of him."

"She loved him," Mary said.

"She used him," Riordan corrected grimly. "If she'd loved him, she would have stayed here where she belonged."

"But she never belonged here . . . I think that's something you were never able to understand. No matter how much she loved your father, your mother would never have been happy on this ranch. It wasn't her environment. As much as your father loved her, didn't you ever wonder why he didn't move to the city to be with her?" Mary answered her own question. "He would have been miserable because he didn't belong there. Their love for each other was the bridge between the two worlds, and it was a very strong one."

"Like a migrating butterfly, mother flew over that bridge every spring and left every fall." His voice was savagely harsh. "I will not be plunged into darkness for nine months of the year the way dad was. I may have inherited his curse for falling in love with butterflies, but I will never marry one!"

The fragile hope that had been building inside Jill began to crumble. It was just as she had told herself last summer. Although Riordan was attracted to her, he also despised her violently.

"Butterflies," Mary murmured with amused disbelief. "You believe Jill is a butterfly?"

"Picture her in your mind, Mary," he sighed bitterly. "Her hair is as golden as the sun and her eyes are as big and as blue as the sky. She's so fragile, I could snap her in two with one hand. Men are drawn to her just like they were drawn to my mother."

"Riordan, you're blind!"

"Oh, no," he declared. "I kept my eyes open all the time so I could see all the traps she laid for me."

"Since when do butterflies have to lay traps?" Jill had to strain to hear the housekeeper's soft voice. "Jill is very beautiful, but she isn't a butterfly. Look at the way she fought for her friend and stood up to you. She's slender and supple like a willow, but not fragile."

In the silence that followed, Jill's mind raced to assimilate Mary's words. Finally she came up with the same verdict. She was not a butterfly. She not only loved Riordan but she loved his home and life as well. She had never needed to feed on the admiration of others to survive as his mother had. Wild elation swept over her.

The silence was shattered by Riordan's snarl. "You don't know what you're talking about!"

Long striding steps were carrying him to the hall-way door where Jill stood. Suddenly she didn't want him to discover she had been there listening. She stepped hurriedly away from the door, intending to retreat to the front of the house, but it was too late. The door was yanked open.

Riordan stopped short.

The harsh lines of anger on his face changed to stunned surprise, but his features were nonetheless forbidding. Jill blinked at him uncertainly. This couldn't be the same man whose voice she had heard state that he loved her. There was not even a flicker of gladness in the wintry silver eyes at the sight of her.

"What are you doing here?" he demanded coldly.

Her fingers tightened convulsively on the packages in her arms. "It's Christmas," she offered in hesitant explanation.

His gaze slid to the gaily wrapped presents. "Get

out, Jill," he said with the same freezing calm. "I don't want anything from you."

Chilled by his cold command, Jill swayed to carry out his order. Then a voice warned that this was her last chance. If she left him now, there would never be another.

"Did you. . . ." She halted to chase the quiver from her voice. "Did you mean it when you said you loved me?"

"You were listening?" A dark brow arched, arrogantly aloof. Jill nodded numbly. "Yes, I meant it," Riordan acknowledged, "but it doesn't change anything."

"It must," she breathed fervently, taking a step toward him, then another, all the while anxiously searching his face for some indication of his love. "I did try to trick you and maneuver you and do all those things you accused me of, but I never intended to let my own emotions become involved. Riordan, you must believe me. I mean, whoever heard of a butterfly coming back in the dead of winter?" She made a feeble attempt at a joke, but it failed miserably as he remained withdrawn. "I never meant to fall in love with you. It just happened. I love you."

He reached out and took the packages from her arms, flipped them onto a table in the hall, then gathered her to him, saying not a word and letting the blazing light in his eyes do all the talking. Covering her mouth with a hungry kiss, he lifted her off the floor and carried her into the living room.

It was much later before anything other than incoherent love words could be spoken. Jill was nestled against his shoulder, the long length of him stretched in a half-sitting position on the sofa. The thudding beat of his heart was beneath her head, the most blissful sound she had ever heard.

"Do you think she really loved him?" Riordan murmured.

Peering through the top of her lashes, Jill could see he was gazing at the portrait. "I think she did. She gave him all the love she had."

His arms tightened around her. "And you, darling? Will you promise to give me all the love you have?"

"Yes," she whispered achingly. Her fingers crept to his face, caressing the rugged features she loved so much. "Oh, Riordan, that will be the easiest promise in the world to keep."

"I'll probably be very jealous and possessive and you'll start to hate me," he smiled wryly.

"Not any more than I shall be." She outlined his hard, passionate mouth with her fingertip and sighed. "I wish I didn't have to leave. Darling, please come home with me. We'll drive together and you can meet my family."

He moved her hand away, tucking a hand under her chin and lifting her head so he could plant a hard kiss on her lips.

"I don't intend to let you out of my sight." His low voice vibrated with emotion, delicious shivers ran over Jill's skin at its intensity. "We'll get married while we're at your parents' and be husband and wife before the New Year comes."

Jill glowed. "Are you sure you want to marry me?"

"Sure?" His gray eyes, warm and vibrantly alive, caressed her face. "Did you think I intended to make another cheap proposition? I admit it was cheap, darling. But that morning I came to your room I knew I had to have you. What I didn't realize was how completely I wanted you . . . forever. That was something I learned in the last six months—painfully, I might add. Besides, I have to marry you to exorcise your ghost from this house. You don't know what it's like to have you haunting my bedroom every night."

"I think I might have an idea," she murmured, snuggling deeper in his arms, unbelievably content. "I can hardly wait to tell Kerry that we're getting married."

"I never expected to beat Todd to the altar," Riordan chuckled.

Her eyes had been half-closed, savoring the dreamlike sensation of being in his arms and loved by him. Her lashes sprang open suddenly, tension darkening the blue shade of her eyes.

"Riordan, what about college?" she breathed uncertainly. "I only have a half a year to go to get my diploma."

He stiffened for an instant, then untangled her from his arms and rolled to his feet, walking to the fireplace. His hand rubbed the back of his neck, ruffling the jet black hair curling near his collar.

"You don't want me to go back, do you?" she said, sitting up and gazing at his broad shoulders sadly.

"No, I don't want you to go back!" Riordan snapped savagely. "I've just found you. How could I possibly want to let you go!"

Jill swallowed tightly. She knew the torment he was going through. A knife was twisting in her own heart. She could guess how much deeper the pain went for him.

"It's all right." She lowered her head, her tawny gold hair swinging forward to hide a selfish disappointment. "I'll quit. I don't mind, really."

"Like hell you will!" He pivoted sharply toward her. "You'll finish college. I'm not going to let you quit."

"You don't know what you're saying." Her head jerked up to stare unbelievingly into his unrelenting gaze.

"It's only for a few months. I'll . . . I'll move into town."

"You'd hate it." Jill shook her head.

"I could stand it." He walked back to the sofa, his hands digging into her shoulders as he pulled her to her feet. "But I couldn't stand being without you, not for a day."

"Nor I you." She cupped his face in her hands. "But I won't let you leave this ranch. I love you too much to ask that of you, Riordan." She breathed in sharply, a compromise suddenly offering itself. "I know what I'll do. I'll transfer my credits to the university in Dillon and drive back and forth every day from the ranch."

His mouth tightened grimly. "And drive me insane with worry about you out alone on the roads!"

Jill slipped her arm around his neck, lifting her face invitingly towards his. "But I'll be home every night, darling."